Back in the mid-eighties, I wrote *Texas Anthem*. It was the first of a family saga set against the western frontier from the end of the Mexican-American War to the turn of the century. *Texas Born* soon followed and carried us forward several years from the events chronicled in *Texas Anthem*. We've watched Big John Anthem become a successful and respected rancher and carve his own empire out of the wilds of West Texas. He has sired two sons and a daughter, all of them mavericks, and a real challenge for their parents as we've discovered. I am pleased that St. Martin's Press is reprinting all five novels in the series.

The Anthem family is a robust collection of men and women shaped by the land, a strong and independent breed, often flawed and perhaps too headstrong, but the kind of folks who will stand for justice, live life to the fullest, and cast a tall shadow.

Rogue River continues the adventures of John Anthem's eldest son, Cole Tyler Anthem. When the woman he loves is shot and left for dead by the notorious Sam Dollard, Cole Anthem turns manhunter, not for gold or fame but to settle a personal score. It is a quest that leads deep into the High Lonesome, into the heart of the Indian wars. Trapped with their backs to the mountains, mortal enemies will be forced to band together against a savage foe. Courage, treachery, lust, and betrayal fill these desperate hours. For Cole Anthem and a handful of brave survivors, escape lies in a

running battle, roaring rapids and a daring, dangerous ride down a river of no return.

* * *

I reckon this is where I'm expected to tell you how I
lived a life of towering adventure, saddle-broke a hundred wild mustangs, pitched a tent in Tibet, hunted
Cape buffalo, served with distinction, rode with the
wind, trampled the wild places and the crooked high-
ways . . . oh, heck with it. That's not me.

I was the kid who sat in the front row of the bal-
cony of the movie theater and spent every Saturday
afternoon with the likes of John Wayne, Burt Lan-
caster, Kirk Douglas, Lee Marvin, Charlton Heston,
Gregory Peck, and the list goes on; a kid who thrilled
to the sight of charging Comanches, saloon brawls,
and shoot-outs in dusty streets, not to mention sword
fights, heroic last stands, dueling pirate ships, and
chariot races. And when I wasn't at the theater, I was
reading the same, yondering by way of the written
word, finding the lost and lonely places, and dreaming
I would one day be the tale-teller, spinning legends on
the wheel of my imagination.

Sure, I've done some things, been some places. But
so have you. All that matters now, my friend, is the
story we share. I have tried to craft these books with a
sense of legend as well as history; finding just the
right blend of thrills, drama, romance, and a dash of
wit. Whether or not I have succeeded is in your hands.

KERRY NEWCOMB
OCTOBER, 2001

ROGUE RIVER

KERRY NEWCOMB

**(PREVIOUSLY PUBLISHED UNDER THE
PSEUDONYM JAMES RENO)**

St. Martin's Paperbacks

PUBLISHER'S NOTE

This book is a work of fiction. Names, characters, places, and incidents either are the product of the author's imagination or are used fictitiously, and any resemblance to actual persons, living or dead, events, or locales is entirely coincidental.

ROGUE RIVER

Copyright © 1987 by James Reno.
"Just a Note from the Author" copyright © 2001 by Kerry Newcomb.

ISBN: 0-312-98122-8

Printed in the United States of America

Signet edition / January 1988
St. Martin's Paperbacks edition / October 2001

St. Martin's Paperbacks are published by St. Martin's Press, 175 Fifth Avenue, New York, NY 10010.

10 9 8 7 6 5 4 3 2 1

*For Patty and Amy Rose
and Paul Joseph—with love.*

I would like to thank Aaron Priest, my agent, and Maureen Baron, my editor at NAL. I hope you don't get tired of reading your names on these pages 'cause I am really grateful for your faith and patience.

Thank you, Joyce Petersen, for typing my manuscripts with never a discouraging word.

And last, thank you, Randolph Scott, for riding the range with dignity and being one of the heroes for this Texas boy. I won't forget.

ROGUE RIVER

★

PROLOGUE

DENVER, 1875

Miss Glory Doolin checked her gun first, and then her makeup. After all, a woman had to have her priorities in order.

The gun was a .36-caliber, single-action Navy Colt, its barrel shortened to allow the weapon to fit in a purse. Glory had compensated for the gun's lesser stopping power by notching the lead tips of her bullets. When fired, the slugs would mushroom and then flatten on impact. They could take a man's arm off at the shoulder.

Glory's face was heavily powdered. She began to add even more rouge to her already bright pink cheeks. Her shoulder-length chestnut hair was drawn back and gathered in a chignon of ringlets at the nape of her neck. The cloying scent of vanilla extract made the interior of the cab almost unbearable. Yet it was necessary. If she intended to pass for a whore, she had to look—and smell—the part. She wrinkled her nose, breathed in the overpowering perfume, and sneezed.

She hoped Sam Dollard would smell her. She wanted him to catch her aroma through the closed door of his hotel room and believe it was a whore waiting to come in. He wouldn't suspect a thing until she pulled the Colt from her drawstring bag and handed him a set of manacles.

Glory glanced out at the snow-blanketed streets of the city and noted men of every conceivable station scurrying through the amber pools of light spreading from each streetlamp and disappearing into the deepening shadows. Where were they bound? For hearth and home—or a game of faro at the nearest saloon? Everyone had a story to tell, her ma had once said. Glory's was simple. She was young and pretty, and she hunted men for the bounty on their heads.

The driver, Burt Olsen, turned and looked in through the cab window at his passenger. He envied the man who would receive her favors tonight. There weren't many truly beautiful women in a rough town like Denver. He pulled the collar of his woolen coat up around his neck, then with his right hand cracked the tip of his long-handled whip over the heads of his matched bay mares. The animals increased their pace and trotted swiftly through the street.

Glory relaxed and let her mind wander. Sam Dollard wasn't just a bastard, she thought, he was a sorry bastard. The seven-hundred-dollar price the state of Kansas had put on Dollard's head for murder of a sheriff didn't mean near as much to Glory Doolin as the fact that Dollard had stopped at a hardscrabble farm long enough to rape a young bride and leave her a widow. Glory, on Dollard's trail, had missed him by a day. She'd stayed to help out all she could before hitting the trail again. It had brought her to this snow-shrouded street in Denver.

Glory pulled her furred cape around her shoulders as the carriage rolled to a stop in front of a three-story brick building. A sign in bold black letters proclaimed: "NUGGET HOUSE." The hotel sat on a busy thoroughfare crowded with dance halls and saloons full of ranch hands, bull whackers, miners, and farmers.

Burt Olsen climbed down from his seat and walked around to open the door. He touched the narrow brim of his hat.

"Here you go, miss." He took Glory's hand and assisted her out of the carriage. He was surprised when she pressed three silver dollars into the palm of his hand.

"Wait for me," Glory said.

"It's mighty cold," Olsen dryly observed, pulling up his coat collar. He grinned as Doolin added another silver coin to those in his hand. " 'Course I've lived in snow all my life. Ain't froze yet." He nodded toward the mares standing obediently at the stone hitching post as if they'd already been tethered. The animals kept their heads down. Snow dusted their coats.

"I won't be long," Glory said.

The driver chuckled and kicked at the hard-packed wheel-rutted earth. "Heck, ma'am. For the likes of you

I'd wait till the icicles hung off'n my chin and I looked like Jack Frost." He handed the dollars back to Glory, except one. "For the horses," he explained. His broad, homely features split in a good-natured grin.

"Why, Mr. Olsen, you're a romantic," Glory said. The driver turned away to hide his blush. He took a couple of canvas oat bags from under his bench seat and brought them around to his mares.

Glory stepped up onto the boardwalk and started toward the door of the hotel. A figure stepped out of the shadowed alley and moved swiftly toward the young woman. Her right hand closed around the gun in her purse.

"Repent, ye fallen angel," cried an old man dressed in the attire of a minister. But his black frock coat and threadbare trousers looked well lived-in. The man's long silvery hair was matted with grime and stuck out in all directions like Medusa's snakes. "The wrath of God shall be visited upon those who follow the depraved path, who sell their flesh for coin and lead others into sin. Woe to thee, O sinner. Woe to thee."

Glory relaxed her grip on the gun in her purse and tried to continue on past the street preacher. The prophet caught her by the arm and thrust a battered Bible in front of her and opened it to a particular section. "Read thou what has befallen Sodom. Learn for yourself what sin has wrought. Great is the wrath of Jehovah and terrible is his swift punishment. Read! Read, O soiled nightingale, lest you lose your divine soul."

The old man reeked of hemp now that he stood close. Glory had no use for zealots, especially ones crazy from the Mexican weed. She was about to brush him aside when a scrap of paper caught her attention in the holy book.

In the glare of a streetlamp she was able to read the crudely scrawled message: *"Dollard in Room 14."*

She looked up at the street prophet and through his mask of grime and dirt she recognized Jaco Roberts, the man to whom she had paid fifty dollars to learn the exact whereabouts of the fugitive Sam Dollard.

Roberts snapped the book shut and, rolling his eyes up into his head, began to speak in tongues. He lurched past and continued down the walkway. Glory glanced over her shoulder at Burt Olsen, who appeared ready to come to her aid. She waved him off and entered the hotel.

No sooner had Glory vanished from sight than Olsen noticed the street preacher whirl around and, shedding the guise of decrepititude, trot back to the hotel's entrance. He rubbed the moisture from the window in the door, peered in for a moment, and then hurried inside.

Olsen scratched his neck beneath his muffler and wondered whether or not he should stick his nose into the situation. After all, none of this was his affair. No matter that his passenger had been prettier than a springtime in the Rockies. No matter . . .

"Aw, hell," he muttered, poised between a north wind and trouble.

* * *

The hall on the second floor was bathed in the smoky
amber light of oil lamps set on tables along the wood-
paneled corridor. Chromolithographs depicting the
Tower of London, various English frigates, and Lon-
don Bridge adorned the walls.

Glory Doolin emerged from the main stairway and
paused a moment to allow her vision to adjust to the
diminished light. To her left were rooms numbered
one through seven; to her right, another stairway and
rooms eight through fourteen.

Sam Dollard's room was at the end of the hall.
Nothing to do now but finish what she had come to
do. The clerk downstairs had assured Doolin, whom
he took for a prostitute, that the "gentleman" in fourteen was awaiting her.

The hall was quiet, save for the murmur of voices
from behind closed doors, muffled conversations, and
softly, a woman's sobs of pain or bliss or both.

Glory lifted the hem of her skirt and started down
the hall. Tension formed a knot in her gut. She tred a
narrow pathway worn in the faded maroon rug that
played out halfway down the hall in a fringe of wine-
colored strands.

"How the hell could you draw that third queen?" a
man complained in a booming voice that rattled door
number nine.

Glory's right hand caught the Navy Colt in her
purse, on pure reflex, and remained there. The door at
the end of the hall loomed gray and solid, like some
massive headstone without a name, only a number.

The tightness in her gut was a familiar feeling; it didn't bother her. In fact, she used such nervousness. Something else bothered her as she reached the end of the hall and raised a perfumed wrist to bang her hand against door fourteen.

A premonition of disaster that the memory of a young Kansas widow overrode.

She knocked on the door, the noise disturbing the empty silence of the hall.

"Ah'm here, honey. Come all the way across town from Ma Crosby's," Glory said in the lilting tones of a jaded coquette. "And Ah'm just frozen to the bone and need someone to come warm me up."

Nothing.

Time flows like molasses in winter. And then the shifting and scrape of an iron bolt sliding back. The creak of hinges and the whisper of wood against the frame as the door opens . . . behind her.

Glory whirled as the first gunshot boomed in the hall. The slug seared her shoulder and left a streak that burned like molten metal on her flesh.

Glory bounced off the closed door behind her as a short broad-shouldered figure stepped from the dark doorway, his gun spewing flame. Another slug ripped into her side. Glory gasped, the impact knocking the wind out of her. She slid to the floor, feeling the blood run down her arm and side. Sam Dollard turned and ran.

The doors in the hallway remained conspicuously closed as the gunman tore down the hall to the stairway. Glory could barely make him out as she struggled to raise the gun still in her cloth purse. Dollard was accosted by a raggedy wraith of a man at the top of the stairs.

"Is she finished?" Jaco Roberts asked of the gunman. "I won't live to spend a dime. She'll know I sold her out. Tell me she's dead."

Dollard shoved the false preacher aside and darted down the stairs, for one brief second outlined in the light from below. Then he vanished.

Jaco Roberts removed his flat-crowned hat and brought a pearl-handled derringer out of the crown.

"Glory . . ." he softly called, his eyes adjusting to the dimly lit hall.

Glory made no reply. She knew she was hurt bad, that Sam Dollard had escaped, she might die, and here was the man directly responsible. Jaco was a wretched little man, without scruples—she should have known better than to trust him.

Her right arm trembled as she braced herself, hoping to God she had the strength to cock the weapon, to pull the trigger.

"Glory . . . Ah," Jaco said, spying her against the wall, a broken rag doll in a bloody dress, but alive, holding her purse out to him. Offering him money to spare her life? "Your money was good, but his was better," Jaco said, raising the derringer. He shrugged. "The purse is mine anyway. Looks like I'll end this night a rich man," he added with a grin, and reached for the drawstring purse.

Glory fired. The flattened slug ripped apart the handbag, obliterated the fingers from Jaco's outstretched hand, and slapped him between the eyes. Roberts toppled backward in a spray of crimson and landed on his back with his arms and legs outstretched and face frozen in death's blank stare.

Glory slumped forward. She heard the clatter of boots on the stairway and felt the floor shudder as another man approached. If it was Sam Dollard, there was nothing she could do about it. Glory didn't have the strength to bring her revolver to bear.

She tensed, waiting for the shot that would finish her. Come on, get it over with, you bastard, she thought.

Suddenly two strong arms encircled her in a rough grasp, and her head settled against a thickly muscled shoulder. She smelled sweat and horses and hard work on the man.

"Good God, miss. Who done this to you?" The voice and the smell belonged to Burt Olsen.

A door opened from one of the other rooms, some brave soul choosing at last to risk life and limb.

"Get a doctor here. Move, damn you!" Olsen shouted. He continued to wrap Glory in his fatherly embrace. "Hold on, miss. I sent for help. Hold on."

Glory tried to thank him. At least she thought it. Things were darker now, harder to see, harder to think. But she had to speak, to tell Burt a name, in case the worst happened.

"What's that, miss? Olsen said, lowering his ear to the woman's mouth. "You want me to what? . . . Yeah, I know the place. Who do I ask for, who do you want me to get?"

Glory's features bunched as the numbness faded
and white-hot pain coursed the length of her side, from
shoulder to toes. She was losing consciousness, the
world was spinning. She seemed to be looking at Burt
Olsen as if from the bottom of a well. His voice was
a garbled echo now, calling to her. She knew what he
was asking, what he had to know, the name of the
man she needed.

Tumbling helplessly into the abyss, Glory summoned the last of her fading strength and screamed
his name. It reached the hall as a whisper.

"Cole . . . Anthem."

1

★

Montana Territory, 1876

There were two things Cole Tyler Anthem especially hated on that bitter cold afternoon in mid-March. One was Sam Dollard, the scout for the Army survey detail, a man Cole believed had led them into a Cheyenne ambush. The other was the chill north wind that numbed his fingers and caused him to fumble with the cartridges as he slid them into the chamber of his Yellowboy Winchester. He cursed the day he had hired on as wrangler for Doc Fleming's survey crew. Cole had only taken the job to keep track of Dollard, who was now wanted by the law in Kansas and Colorado. Posters out of Denver claimed attempted murder. *Attempted*, hell. He's getting us all killed today, Cole thought as he ducked a red-tipped arrow arcing toward him. It thwacked into the makeshift barricade of timber Cole was hiding behind. "Kill us all," he thought aloud as he stared at the mass of Red Shield warriors streaming out of the wooded hillside.

The Red Shields were one of the most feared of all the Cheyenne warrior societies, and certainly the most fearsome-looking. They colored their flesh with red war paint and smeared the hooves of their mounts as well. Their war shields were crimson-tinted hide, and several carried twelve-foot-long spears, the blades blood-red. The braves wore buffalo hats, the horns also tipped with what looked to be dried blood. Such warriors took no wives, had no families. They lived only for battle.

"Well, enjoy yourselves, you bastards," Cole muttered as he finished loading his carbine.

"Goddamn that Dollard. Calls himself a scout? Lawd, he couldn't find snow in a blizzard," a man spoke up on Cole's left. Anthem rolled on his side and recognized a young private by the name of Meadows. The soldier clutched his Springfield breechloader and stared at the woods.

"I seen him—seen Medicine Bear. He's the one yonder with the bear claws hung around his neck. Never thought we'd run into him. And now he's gonna kill us!" Private Meadows rose to his knees, his face filled with terror.

"I saw Doc Fleming killed. See him, there yonder." Meadows lifted a trembly hand. "Lieutenant's dead too." His eyes widened.

"Oh my God," he groaned. Cole reached for him, but the soldier pulled away and struggled to his feet. He stepped over the log and was stopped in his tracks by a swarm of lead slugs that tore into his thin, bony frame as the Red Shields across the clearing opened up with their rifles. His whole body shuddered at the impact. A bullet flattened against his side, and he sat down on Anthem's log.

Meadows' expression was one of surprise and disbelief as he looked slowly down at his ravaged torso. Then his eyes dimmed and he pitched forward off the log, breaking off a branch and ripping the sleeve of his tattered blue coat. A small gush of bright blood stained the trampled snow as he stiffened and died.

Cole did the only thing he could for Meadows. He squeezed off a shot at the braves massing on the edge of the woods. Nearly twenty warriors waited among the shadows of the lodgepole pines. Cole's breath steamed from between his frost-cracked lips in a low whistle.

Suddenly there was quiet in the clearing. The tiny area of the mountain took on a tranquillity whose benevolence was denied only by the scattered dead. The survey's campsite was littered with corpses. Here and there a body stirred, an arm rose out of the snow and as quickly settled back. Someone groaned, another poor soul took up the mournful song. The onslaught had lasted but a few minutes. Medicine Bear had led a red tide of more than forty warriors that swept through the unsuspecting party's loose circle of wagons, trampling and killing most of the command, before they were driven off to the line of trees about fifty yards away. Spirals of smoke rose in the cold, wet air as the wagons burned, and a hushed expectancy settled over the scene.

Away from the wagons and safely hidden in the

shadows of the lodgepole pines, Medicine Bear, astride bald-faced pinto, was deciding whether or not to risk another full-scale attack or try to pick the remaining *ve-ho-e* off from the trees. It was a risky business. The first assault had cost half a dozen braves, and he was loath to lose any more to the soldiers' Springfields. On the other hand, the battle had whetted his appetite. The more scalps he carried to the great gathering of Sioux and Cheyenne, the greater his honor and prestige. Could Sitting Bull or Gall or Crazy Horse boast of the first victory over the white-eyes?

Life came to the smoked-filled clearing as the living struggled to more comfortable positions and looked around to see who was still alive. Cole Anthem, behind his barricade between two of the wagons, checked the remains of the survey party. The bodies of Doc Fleming and his accompanying surveyors were sprawled in the snow, half-concealed by their trampled tents. Out of a military detail of twelve men he counted five living and able to fight. He added two surviving teamsters to his count. Seven, and Cole made eight. Eight men and Lord only knew how many Cheyenne.

A flurry of snowflakes from the frigid, colorless sky settled on his neck. Cole shivered, and not only from the cold. The situation looked pretty hopeless. He had no illusions about the camp's ability to withstand another attack.

Anthem drew his revolver, a Colt .45, opened the cylinder, and removed a cartridge. He bit off the bullet—an act that loosened a couple of molars—resealed the cartridge with wadding, and returned it to the cylinder. He placed the weapon close at hand on the log.

He cursed Sam Dollard again for leading the detail into such a trap. Where the hell was Dollard anyway? He cursed Doc Fleming and the military for the fool need to map these mountains. And he didn't forget to curse himself for hiring on as a wrangler.

"I'm the biggest fool of all," he muttered. He should never have waited for Dollard, but taken the man and not worried about the consequences of Dollard's being attached to the military. Revenge and a seven-hundred-dollar bounty weren't worth getting scalped for.

He took stock of the situation. Eight men couldn't hold their position. The makeshift barricade he was hiding behind was rapidly disappearing in the fire, and it now barely concealed his lanky frame. Anthem was a blunt, square-featured individual with harsh blue eyes and straw-colored hair hanging to his neck. A thick yellow mustache hid his upper lip. Grim-faced, he turned to the men around him.

"There's a creek and a stand of trees yonder," he called out. "At least we won't have to die in the flames."

The teamsters and soldiers glanced behind them at the timber, a fringe of oak and willow lining the creek bank.

"Sounds good to me," one of the teamsters said. It looked to be about a hundred feet away.

"It's a sight more cover than this barrel of apples."

Sergeant Danny McKane spoke up from amongst the soldiers. The sergeant was a gray-haired, slightly built Irishman. Gregarious to a fault, he could brawl in the best tradition of the sons of Eire. "And I'd as soon let these red devils send me under as roast in their fire."

McKane scratched his stubbly chin, tugged the ragged mustache he wore, then chuckled aloud.

"I run ol' Medicine Bear out of Fort Conrad once," the sergeant said. "Drunk on settler's whiskey he was, and braggin' about how he was a big man among the Cheyenne. And I had to go and put me boot to his backside."

"Better hope Medicine Bear has a bad memory," Anthem called out.

"It don't look it! Here they come!" one of the soldiers shouted.

"Head for the creek, lads," McKane yelled, and scrambled to his feet.

Cole looked toward the hillside in time to see the Red Shields streaming down the forested slope at a gallop. The hooves on their war ponies trampled the snow and drummed upon the earth like an army cadence. War cries filled the air and smoke blossomed from the ends of their rifles.

Red lances lowered as braves vied with one another to be the first to impale a fleeing soldier.

Cole stood, loosed a shot, then, remembering, grabbed his revolver and headed for the creek. He had barely cleared the circled wagons when the Red Shields charged into the smoky clearing. Cole realized with a sickening feeling that he would never reach the creek. He ran a dozen yards out into the trampled buffalo grass, spun around, and dropped to one knee, momentarily losing his foot in the moist snow.

He snapped the Winchester up to his shoulder. The carbine seemed an extension of himself. Its brass frame gleamed even in the dull light as Cole steadied the weapon, drawing a bead on the curtain of smoke that obscured the campsite.

A Cheyenne brave materialized alongside a burning wagon. He came riding at a gallop, his warpainted physique and his shield and lance that appeared to be dipped in blood, a chilling sight. Cole shifted his aim, squeezed off a shot. The warrior pitched from horseback. A dozen more apparitions took his place. Twenty, thirty braves, Medicine Bear himself, charged out of the smoke.

Some of the soldiers reached the trees. Others took what cover they could find. One of the teamsters, armed with a Spencer, moved up abreast of Cole's Winchester, and the two weapons sent a flurry of lead that downed horses and riders. The attackers parted and swept past the two men.

"I wish I was back in Texas," Cole said, his voice lost in the rattle of gunfire.

Behind him, guns began to speak back at the creek. The crack-crack-crack of the Springfields and the screams of the dying spoke volumes of the desperate struggle taking place.

There was no time to listen. Levering spent cartridges, cocking, and firing took every second. Cole barely had time to aim, but that was of little consequence, for he fired almost instinctively at the quickly moving figures rushing past.

"Anthem!" The teamster shouted a warning. Cole heard him and swung the carbine in the direction the man had indicated, but the mounted warrior bore down on him fast, charging through the tall grass, less than a stride away.

Cole instinctively fired, batted the Indian's spear point, and tried to dodge the horse, but failed. The animal slammed into Cole and knocked him backward into the snow. A hoof narrowly missed his skull as the horse galloped past, its rider doubled over in pain and clinging to the mane.

Cole gasped for air and struggled to maintain consciousness. He pushed himself aright, realized he was unarmed, and began numbly searching for his carbine.

The air suddenly grew thick with the whir of arrows, spiced with an angry buzz of bullets fired from the guns the Indians had traded for. The teamster with the Spencer was desperately slamming shells into his repeater when three arrows ended his frantic attempt. He dropped the rifle, his face contorted with pain as he fell forward into the frozen mud and snow and gave a long, last agonizing cry.

Cole remembered his revolver, dragged it from the holster. The gunfire back toward the river stopped, which meant the fighting there was over. In fact, a stillness had settled over the entire meadow. The moment had come. The Cheyenne braves were returning from the creek to join an ever-increasing circle about the lone remaining white man in the snow-patched clearing.

Snow began to drift in lazy flurries from the slate-gray clouds that formed an ominous low ceiling overhead.

Cole checked his weapon, positioning the cylinder until the blank was in line with the cocked hammer. He waited, wincing as he inhaled and his chest expanded, his bruised ribs protesting with the effort.

The circle of braves tightened as one brave in particular broke off from the others. He was a lithe, muscular individual with his solemn features hidden behind a layer of garish war paint. A bear-claw necklace hung down his chest. Medicine Bear brandished a twelve-foot spear, and raised the weapon so that Cole could see the freshly severed head impaled on the flint blade.

Cole recognized the head of one of the troopers who had fled with the sergeant toward the creek. The circling braves stopped and turned their horses toward the man in the middle.

Medicine Bear raised up on horseback and snapped the spear shaft forward. The head flew through the air, landed in the snow, and rolled to within a few feet of the white man, who jumped away despite himself. The circle of Red Shield warriors exploded in laughter. Anthem flushed. He didn't like being ridiculed.

"White man," shouted Medicine Bear, "what is your name?" His voice reverberated across the meadow.

"Cole Tyler Anthem," the bounty hunter replied.

"Cole Tyler Anthem," I think I will take your head for my lance," the war chief said. "I think it will bring me much good fortune."

"It hasn't brought me any," Cole replied sourly.

Medicine Bear considered the man's reply, caught the sense of Cole's jest, and began to laugh. He repeated the exchange in Cheyenne for the benefit of his braves, who laughed and shook their weapons at the circled man.

"Die well, *ve-ho-e*, and we will sing of your deeds around our campfire even while we eat your heart," Medicine Bear called out.

His war horse pranced and fought the reins, reared and pawed the air. Medicine Bear loosed a wild cry. Raven feathers adorning his buffalo cap splayed out, adding to his fearful appearance.

The surrounding braves took up their war chief's cry. The noise was deafening, chilling.

Cole stood his ground, facing the war chief of the Red Shields bearing down on him. He waited, wanting to be certain that Medicine Bear and the rest of the warriors could see him.

A shouting horde of savages, drumming hooves, a twelve-foot lance in the hands of a fanatic warrior—the entire scene froze for a second, as if time itself had paused. Cole smiled and raised the revolver to his head.

"Sorry, fellows," he said. And he fired the gun into the side of his skull.

2

Darkness. A motionless void. Silence. Nothing. And then something. A pinprick of light, and with it, pain. Cole focused on both, the light and the hurt. He clung to both in desperation, knowing to lose his grip meant a free-fall into a never-ending abyss.

A voice exhorted him to hang on, hang on, not to let go. It was his own voice.

A few seconds or maybe an eternity later (for who could tell the difference in such a place), darkness became a warm, bright memory. Two boys, all of thirteen, out hunting deer in the shadow of Mescalero Lookout appeared—Cole Anthem and his twin, Billy, waited patiently beneath the slow crawl of a lazy Texas sun. At the base of the slope in a dry wash, a mule deer hesitated and Cole fired.

"Got him!" Cole shouted, scrambling past his brother to hurry down the gully. When he reached his kill, Cole blooded himself, dipping his fingers into the gaping wound left by the slug.

The image faded, became another kind of blooding,

the carnage of battle. Union and Confederate soldiers sighting one another through black clouds of gunsmoke. Minie balls swarmed like bees. And everywhere lay the twisted, wrecked, and ruptured bodies of the wounded and slain.

Pain again. Cole gasped. The scene changed yet once more, and he was a lone young man wandering the West, a remnant of war. Too proud to return penniless and ragged to Luminaria, his father's ranch, Cole had nothing but his pride. Then, after being braced in a dusty street in a Kansas town, he had acquired something else. Reward money and a reputation as a "bad 'un to cross" despite his youth.

Now the memories came flashing past, almost too swiftly to recognize. John Anthem, his father, broad-shouldered and bullnecked and true. Rose Anthem, Cole's mother, regal and graceful and spirited as a wild colt, high-strung as his sister, Rachel, though not as rash. Were anything to happen to Big John Anthem, Cole had no doubt but that the "Yellow Rose" could hold the Anthem domain together.

There had been a homecoming. Billy had gotten himself into trouble and it took a man like Cole Anthem to set things right for his twin. By then Cole had gained another sobriquet as well: Men called him "Yellowboy" for his skill with the brass-framed Winchester '66 that was never far from his fingertips. He was a hunter of men—a bounty hunter. It was a profession he had grown accustomed to. And so he had drifted once again, this time heading north to the mountains and the lure of their vast summits, the high lonesome.

He had hoped to find his fortune there among the lofty ranges and wild free places. He'd hoped to find whatever it was his restless spirit seeked. He never thought his quest would end this way.

Cole opened his eyes and stared up at the gun-metal-gray sky. Sparse snowflakes settled on his cheek, forehead, and bloody, burned scalp. He managed to wriggle his fingers and toes and was relieved to find himself in one piece. So, his ruse had worked. A Cheyenne warrior never touched one who had taken his own life. Suicide was the worst kind of deed, and only evil could be gained from such an encounter.

Cole noticed his body was surrounded by arrows that had been shot into the earth, and he imagined the rage of Medicine Bear when his victim had so cheated him of an honorable kill. They had probably hoped to pen Cole's bad medicine in with the makeshift stockade of arrows.

Cole groaned. His head throbbed and as he reached up, gingerly to examine the wound he had inflicted on himself, his arm felt incredibly heavy. His fingertips probed the powder-burned flesh on his face and picked bloody wadding out of the grisly-looking but superficial wound. The punctured flesh had already caked over.

As Cole raised himself up on his elbows and viewed a crazy, tilting world, he caught a glimpse of his Winchester and converted Colt, bad medicine weapons the Red Shields had left behind. So he had cheated death. Now all he had to do was pull himself to cover and build a fire before he froze lying there in the settling snow.

No problem, he thought encouragingly. Damn, his head hurt like hell. And what was all this blackness creeping in from the border of his vision? He had tricked Medicine Bear only to die from exposure out here in the meadow! The world darkened, careened on its side. *No! I will not faint! I say no!*

Anthem pitched backwards, unconscious. The snowfall increased and flake by feathery white flake began to bury him.

3
★

It was still snowing when Anthem awoke again. The flakes settled on his lacerated scalp and swollen temple, melted, and slid down his face and neck. He didn't mind the discomfort because it meant he was still alive. Even the pain of his head wound was a cause for happiness. It reinforced the fact that once more he had risen out of death's abyss.

Gradually his vision cleared. The smoldering hulks of the wagon sent pale wisps of smoke spiraling up toward the heavy ceiling of gray clouds. The body of a dead horse steamed as it lost its last bit of heat.

Cole tried to sit up but the back of his wool coat was frozen to the ground. As he strained against the invisible shackles of ice, his stomach turned from the effort and he almost vomited. Massing what shaky strength he could, he gave a loud cry and wrenched free of the frozen bonds that held him.

"Lord above!" someone exclaimed.

Cole fumbled for his revolver and turned to see a twenty-year-old black man in mud-spattered coat and trousers back away in horror. He snapped up his Springfield carbine, pointed it at Anthem, and squeezed the trigger. But he had forgotten to cock the gun.

A second figure threw his slender form into the black man's Springfield, knocking the weapon aside.

"Jesus Christ!" Sergeant Danny McKane exclaimed. "Cole, I sure hope you ain't dead."

"No, and I don't intend to be," Cole said feebly. "That is if it's all right with Ben there."

The black man, Ben Wheatley, lowered his gun and looked at the ground in embarrassment.

"Jumpin' Jehoshaphat, by me mother's sweet tears but it's good to see another white face; alive, I mean. Uh, no offense, Wheatley," the sergeant exclaimed, hurrying to Cole's side. His boots sank and slipped in the settling snow.

"No offense taken," Wheatley replied in a thoughtful tone of voice. Ben had been Doc Fleming's assistant and could boast of far better schooling than any of the men around him. He tolerated the sergeant's mild slur because he saw no point in instigating a quarrel now. "I'm sorry, Cole. Lucky for you I'm handier with a surveyor's glass than a rifle." The black man brushed his short-brimmed hat back, rubbed his forehead, and sighed in relief.

"Well, I figured y'all for dead as well." Anthem grinned ruefully.

"I was washing some of my clothes down by the creek bank when they hit," Wheatley said. "I didn't have a gun. I've no use for violence, being a peaceable man. So I hid."

McKane shivered and, reaching down, helped the bounty hunter to stand. "Me and a few of the lads made it to the creek for a last stand." The sergeant doffed his campaign hat and ran a callused hand through his gray hair. "The redskins took out after us and killed everyone but me. I faked getting killed, then swam out into the pond back yonder and hid out in a beaver's lodge. Found Ben there, too. The injuns were so busy with the others they plumb forgot to come back and look for me. But then, me sainted mother says I was born with a charm."

McKane fumbled for his canteen and passed it on to Cole, who took a swallow and reacted in surprise at the fiery liquid cauterizing his throat. Warmth spread to his limbs.

"That's pure Irish whisky, Cole," McKane chuckled. "Water's fine to hide under but I'd sure hate to have to drink it." McKane gave a low whistle. "You're lucky them red heathens didn't carve you up like the other lads. Reckon they just got bored."

Cole managed an ironic grin. "They didn't get bored and forget me, Sergeant. Most Indians won't come near a man who takes his own life. Bad medicine. Even his possessions will bring bad luck. That's why my guns are still here." He managed a hesitant step, leaning on the sergeant.

McKane seemed confused. "Yessir. But what's that got to do with you?"

"Everything, Sergeant," replied Anthem. "I'm a

dead man. I shot myself during the fight." He gestured to the wound on his head.

Ben Wheatley sucked in his breath and muttered "Uh-oh" and began wondering if he was in the company of a madman. He retrieved a saddlebag of provisions he'd managed to scrounge from the gutted wagons as Cole explained about the blank cartridge.

"T'weren't a bad idea at that." McKane nodded sagely. "Be surprised if the Army didn't adopt the idea. Yessir, shoot yourself in the head and live to fight another day."

"Look here," Ben snapped. "If you two gentlemen don't mind, maybe we can find some shelter and get the hell away from here before any more Cheyenne show up." The young man's voice rose in intensity. "We could all wind up butchered like . . . like . . ."

McKane abruptly turned and headed for Fleming's assistant. He jerked the surveyor around with a rough twist of his arm.

"You be getting ahold of yourself now, Ben Wheatley. None of us is looking to die, but if it's in the cards there's nothing to do but play the hand we're dealt."

Wheatley nodded.

Cole stepped up and clapped the youth on the shoulder, forcing himself to sound more optimistic than he felt. "Listen, Ben. We're alive. And we're staying that way," he said. "I've no intention of dying twice in the same day." He paused, tried to will away the pain in his skull, then added, "C'mon."

They needed much more food. They needed fire and

shelter to survive the night. Cole headed for the creek, weaving like a drunkard. His head hurt like blazes. But at least he had a head.

Behind him, Ben Wheatley wiped a forearm across his ebony features and in a deep, melodic voice bemoaned his fate. "I have the distinct feeling I shall never see Boston, Massachusetts, again," he said with a sigh of resignation.

"Well, there you go, bucko," Sergeant McKane said, taking a nip from his canteen and forging ahead. "You've something to be grateful for after all."

Ben Wheatley sighed again, finding little amusement in the sergeant's observation. Truly, Ben thought, I have fallen on hard times. Doc Fleming, his mentor and benefactor, was dead. Poor Doc, a fervent abolitionist who had taken in a young runaway slave boy and had given him a proper home and an education. Ben had studied mathematics and physics; he could play Beethoven's Piano Sonata in C Minor and quote Shakespeare. But he knew very little of survival.

The black man paused and gazed up at the cold gray sky, shivering in his wet clothes as he realized all his education, all his talents were now for naught. Ben looked at the receding figures of McKane and Anthem. What was he to do in this wilderness. Survive! Up ahead, Cole turned at the edge of the trees and waved toward the black man.

And Ben Wheatley, lately of Boston, hefted his rifle and satchel of provisions and hurried after.

4

★

Night found the three men holed up in a shallow cave on the side of the mountain, a good half mile from the site of the massacre. They had uprooted some underbrush to mask the entrance to the cave. The chamber itself ran about ten feet back and was little more than a depression in the ridge's stony face. Still, it kept them out of the wind and they were grateful.

McKane and Wheatley had gathered pine needles and deadwood and brought them to Cole. He tore a couple of lengths of fringe from his buckskin jacket and tied them together to make a bowstring long enough to fit a bow two feet in length. He used a twelve-inch willow stick for a drill, and set the point of the drill in a depression he had gouged out of a flat piece of birchbark. He wrapped the bow-string once around the drill and began sawing back and forth. The wrap of the string caused the drill to spin. The spinning motion of the drill created enough friction to produce a tiny flame at its pointed end. The sergeant added a few dry twigs and pieces of bark and soon coaxed the flames into a full-fledged campfire.

The back of the cave reflected the warmth of the fire. The smoke drifted upward, found a break in the underbrush blocking the entrance, and rose into the cold night air.

Cole added a couple of pine logs to the fire, hoping to build up the blaze enough for everyone to grab some rest.

McKane stirred and propped himself upon his elbow. "You reckon it's safe havin' a fire, Cole? Them redskins'll smell us out for sure."

"We'll freeze to death if we don't," Cole said. "No, it isn't safe but then nothing is, out here." The bounty hunter ran a hand through his straw-colored hair and scratched his scalp. "Since the snow's still falling, Medicine Bear and his bucks are probably holed up same as us."

"I am just grateful to be warm," Ben Wheatley said in his cultured voice. He had stripped off his shirt and was drying it by the fire. His upper torso gleamed like chiseled obsidian in the firelight.

The fire served many purposes. It had been hours since the men had eaten and they were ravenously hungry. Anthem had opened a couple of tins of beans Wheatley had recovered from the wagons, and set them into the coals on the perimeter of the fire. Too, McKane and Wheatley had swam in the creek and Cole had lain in the snow. While their clothes dried and the beans heated, the men gnawed a few leathery strips of beef jerky. Hardtack and beans finished the meal.

We're fed and warm enough to live through the night, Cole thought. Tomorrow will have to take care of itself. He rolled up in his coat on a bed of green boughs, closed his eyes, and listened to the wind as it moaned through the trees like the wail of lost souls. . . .

Cole shivered and tried to picture something else. Glory Doolin, yes, now there was a woman with lips sweet as wine and muscled thighs to hold a man tight and let him ride and ride. And no fancy debutante but a real woman, quick with a pretty smile or a Navy Colt. She was a bounty hunter, one who seldom made mistakes. But she had made one. She had tried to bring in Sam Dollard alive.

An image formed: a memory of a hospital room in Denver and Glory Doolin, her chestnut hair drawn back and concealed in a sleeping cap, looking plain and tired and hurt. She was asleep and Cole didn't wake her. He kissed her forehead and stole from the room and found a bespectacled little man who called himself Doctor Schaefer.

"Will she live?" Cole asked.

"She's strong," Schaefer said, clearing his throat. "Yes. But she is a lucky girl. Shot in the back. Who would do such a thing. Mmmm, mmmm, mmmm."

"A man named Sam Dollard," Cole replied. The trail was already getting cold. He'd have to hurry. Anthem dropped a stack of gold eagles in Schaefer's hand and ordered him to give her the best of care.

It had taken Cole three months to track down Sam Dollard, only to find him under the protection of the

Army. But Anthem had been patient, he'd bided his time. He had even hired onto Doc Fleming's crew just to keep track of Dollard. And now, thanks to Medicine Bear, Cole had lost his man.

Embers crackled and popped. The wind kept up its keening lament and Cole drifted into a fitful sleep, burdened with worries of the past and the hazards to come.

Morning dawned bright and clear, and with the glow of sunshine came a gleam of optimism. Even Ben Wheatley, for all the despair he had felt the night before, began to consider their situation precarious but not entirely hopeless.

Cole and Sergeant McKane were hunkered down at the edge of the cave, studying a crude map McKane had drawn in the snow. Their breath clouded as they spoke. The valley beyond wore a mantle of sun-sparkled snow. The boughs of lodgepole pine, aspen, and fir drooped under the weight of snow. Gray squirrels scampered across the drifts and darted up nearby trunks whenever one of the men at the mouth of the cave made an overt motion.

"Now, here's about where we are," McKane said. "As close as I can figure." He made an "X" in the snow. "To the north is the Rogue, which cuts over to the Marias and, following the river pass, heads on down to Fort Conrad. Now, I heard from a good fellow that Major Busby was planning on establishing a post in from the Rogue, right in the heart of the Cheyenne and Blackfoot hunting grounds."

"To provoke the tribes into an all-out war?"

"Only way to have the government open up this territory is to have the Cheyenne and Sioux and Blackfeet run head on into the troops."

"Busby is crazy," Cole said in disgust.

"True enough," conceded the sergeant. "But I suppose that son of a bitch, uh . . . beggin' your pardon, sir, that Major Busby oughta be warned. There's some good lads with him. If Busby's to the north of here and Medicine Bear joins up with any more Injuns, well, things might turn nasty."

Anthem frowned. "I don't know. It's hard to tell where Medicine Bear is headed. We could have seen the whole raiding party or it could have been a small part of a much bigger band. Damn, I wish I knew what's happened to Dollard." Cole didn't elaborate on the real reason he wanted to know the scout's whereabouts.

Both men sat in silence. Wheatley held his peace, looking expectantly from one to the other. At last he cleared his throat and interjected himself into the conversation.

"If it's any help, Doc Fleming had orders to rendezvous with Major Busby in the middle of the month, to oversee the construction of a military outpost. We were to meet at a place called Morgan's Landing."

"I know where it is," McKane said. The Irishman fished in his pocket for a pipe, then remembered he had lost it the day before. "But it's gonna take us a good four or five days careful walkin'. And that's if we don't run into those Red Shields."

Wheatley's spirits began to sag once more. He cursed the day Doc Fleming had forsaken his Boston practice to follow a vocation as a cartographer and surveyor of the lands in the West. Poor Fleming, his thirst to be at the forefront of history, to experience adventure, to seek fame and fortune in the untamed wilds of the western lands had brought him an early grave. And stranded Ben Wheatley with little hope of a better fate.

"Maybe we won't have to walk." Anthem's voice jarred the black man from his self-pity. The Texan had Wheatley's complete attention once again.

Anthem drew his knife and gestured to a blank area in the snow halfway between their estimated position and the landing. "Isn't there a trading post out here? A hardcase and his family that the Indians don't bother?"

McKane's eyes lit up. "The Hammonds! Why, blast my soul, why didn't I think of it. Ol' man Hammond and his boys trade goods for horses and pelts. Zack and Jay Lee are a pair of hellions. Raised wild they are. But I hear that new wife he brought up from St. Louis is a looker." McKane winked at Anthem. "She sets a handsome table, too. And it's only a couple of days walk."

"Do you think the Indians will leave them be?" Wheatley chimed in.

Cole stood and returned his knife to the sheath sewn onto the inside of his boot. He glanced toward McKane for a reply.

"I don't see why not," the Irishman said. "Gus

Hammond's been a pretty good friend to the red devils."

"Maybe too good," Cole added. "Some of the Red Shields were armed with repeating rifles. Somebody had to have sold them those guns." Anthem stepped into the cave and emerged a moment later with his Winchester in hand.

"We might find food and horses," the bounty hunter said, his blue eyes hardening. "Then again, we might find Medicine Bear himself."

The ice-crusted snow crackled like a gunshot as Cole Anthem took the first step on a journey that lead north to the Hammond place . . . and safety or disaster.

Two miles from the cave farther down the valley, Medicine Bear raised his hands and sang in prayerful thanks to the All-Father for the warmth of the sun, for clear weather, for banishing the Cold Maker. He sang to Morning Star, for the Cheyenne were the people of the Morning Star. He knew the Above Ones heard his prayers and were pleased.

> *"Ha-haeya-hey. Good is the warm sky.*
> *Strong is my spirit when I find my enemy.*
> *Glad is my heart, for the way is*
> *clear and the path is true."*

Medicine Bear's voice carried to the hills across the valley floor and reverberated from the glacier-carved ridges. Twenty yards downslope and into timber line, the rest of the warrior band listened and waited.

A brave named Raven sat amidst his companions and searched through the clothes stolen from the wagons, looking for a blue jacket to fit him. Raven was a stout, solidly built young man. Though not bright, he was a veritable berserker in battle and had slain many enemies in his frenzy. His brother, High-Backed Wolf, had just ridden into camp, having seen the smoke of the Cheyenne cookfires drifting above the treetops.

Raven at last abandoned his search with a scowl. His brother, a smaller young hothead eager to win honor for himself in the coming war with the *ve-ho-e*, laughed at Raven's antics. The other braves looked on in awe that High-Backed Wolf should ridicule his dangerous and unpredictable brother.

"Poor Raven, you will have to kill many soldiers before you find one big enough to have a coat to cover you."

"Maybe I will have to kill all of them," Raven grumbled, and pulled his buckskin shirt over his torso. "I may not have a soldier coat to show for my trouble, but at least I have taken many scalps in battle." Raven pointed to his freshly decorated war lance, his dark features split in a grin. "You did not even ride with us. So tell us, you pretty one, what honor have you won for yourself?"

High-Backed Wolf endured the laughter of those around him in silence. Let them have their way. Until he had taken up the red shield he had courted many girls and had never failed to lure one into his blanket. "I have ridden far and fast and scouted the soldier camps where they build another of their *mena-e* [high-walled corrals] to hide behind."

"And did you count coup?" a stern voice inquired. The brothers turned to see Medicine Bear striding toward them. The war chief had seen twenty-eight summers come and go. He had waited and watched for his chance to assert his authority among the Cheyenne people. When word reached him that the Sioux and Cheyenne nations were gathering at the valley of the Little Big Horn to drive the white men out of the sacred mountains, Medicine Bear knew his moment had come. Many tribes and warrior societies had already gone to camp along the Little Big Horn River. But not the Red Shields. Not yet.

"No one saw me, as you wished," High-Backed Wolf replied.

"It is good," Medicine Bear said. He searched the faces around him and saw only admiration. "We have been the first to strike the soldiers. We will find them where they think to build another fort in our mountains and we will drive them out. And when we ride to the great gathering, to the lodges of Sitting Bull, Crazy Horse, Gall, and American Horse, they will sing of our victories."

The braves surrounding him loosed a wild chorus of yells and war whoops, firing their rifles into the sky. The fusillade startled the horses and crackled sharply in the cold, brittle air.

Medicine Bear reveled in their outcry. He walked out of the circle of warriors and motioned for Raven and High-Backed Wolf to follow him. The two brothers immediately put aside their differences and trotted after their leader.

"Tell all you have seen," Medicine Bear said once they were well away from the others. A breeze blew strands of long black hair across his features. He wore a lone eagle feather in the single braid framing the left side of his face. Clad only in a blanket and leggings, his lithe, muscular body bore the scars of the sun dance ritual. It had been during this long night of pain that he had the first vision of his mighty destiny.

After High-Backed Wolf had recounted every aspect of his mission, Medicine Bear turned to Raven, who waited obediently for instructions. His deep-set eyes betrayed his eagerness, his short muscular frame was tensed. He was ready to ride; inaction did not suit him.

"You will go to the Hammond trading post with your brother. Take all of those of our number who do not yet have rifles. The old man will have the guns for which we gave him gold. When you have the guns, ride on to the crazy woman's on the river. When I attack the soldier coats who try to build their fort in our hunting grounds, some may flee and try to escape in the crazy woman's boat. Do not let this happen. We wait here for Sacred Horse, who brings his warriors to join me in attacking the soldier coats. When we have finished with them, we will join you and the others at the river." Medicine Bear finished and turned away.

"I will stop them," Raven bragged. He thumped his thick chest, then strutted back toward camp, full of his self-importance. High-Backed Wolf lingered for a moment, then started to follow the path his brother had already plowed through the snow.

"Wolf cub," Medicine Bear said softly, his face firm. "Do not let your brother near the white man's firewater."

High-Backed Wolf nodded in understanding. His brown eyes, slender nose, and thin lips were set. Medicine Bear hoped that the young brave would prove equal to his task. The war chief of the Red Shields had plans and would curse those who caused them to go awry.

5

★

Zack Hammond took another bite of his stepmother's cold fried chicken and waited for his father to show himself. Zack was a young man of average height and wiry physique. He ate constantly and never seemed to add an inch to his girth, unlike his older brother, Jay Lee, who had a roll of fat around his middle. Zack scratched the dimple in the middle of his chin and then sank his teeth into the chicken leg.

"He shown himself yet?" Becca Hammond asked as she emerged from the kitchen with a mug of steaming coffee. Becca was a round-hipped redhead, wholesome if a bit fatigued. She wore a man's flannel shirt that strained to cover her breasts, and the canvas trousers she wore clung to her shapely thighs. Her hair was pulled back and tightly fastened with a black ribbon.

"Did you hear this buffalo gun speak?" Zack answered her with a question of his own. "When it does, you'll be a widow."

"What if you miss?" Jay Lee asked. He was the

same height as his brother but potbellied, and a scraggly brown beard barely concealed his double chin. His brown hair was prematurely thin whereas Zack's grew full and thickly curled.

Becca had been a mail-order bride hoping to escape a life of poverty and servitude in St. Louis. But she had never felt any love or passion for Gus Hammond, who was twenty years older and a rough-housing whiskey drinker with a dislike of people and a nasty temper. She fancied Zack and let him know it.

Gus had been in a particularly nasty mood of late because the latest shipment of Henry rifles for the Cheyenne had been held up at Morgan's Landing.

"I said, what if you miss?" Jay Lee repeated, walking over to the front door where Zack balanced the Sharps buffalo gun on its stand.

Zack patted the heavy octagon barrel of the .50-caliber rifle and looked askance at his brother. "Sheeit, Jay Lee. I been hunting buffalo since I could drag this ol' cannon around. You ever known me to miss?"

"Pa's a sight smaller than a buffalo."

"Not to me he ain't," Zack replied. It seemed to Zack that Gus Hammond had spent all his life trying to whip his boys into line, first with a leather strap and then with his fists.

"Maybe we could just tie him up and leave him," Jay Lee said, offering an argument that Zack had rejected better than a week ago. "What with his gold, we could get far away."

Becca moved to Zack's side and fixed Jay Lee with an indolent gaze. "He'd find us. And it wouldn't be pretty when he did," said the redhead. "Now, leave your brother be." She looked at Zack, leaned down, and kissed the back of his neck. "Zack knows what he's doing."

Zack grinned at her. The smell of her aroused him. The way her breasts brushed against his arm didn't hurt either.

"I know that," Jay Lee said. "But look at it this way. Pa said them injuns are gonna be crazy mad when they show up and he doesn't have the rifles he promised them. And having a wagonload of whiskey ain't gonna set things right." Jay Lee stroked his chin, hitched up his pants, cleared his throat, and began to pace, as if he was a lawyer arguing a case. "We leave Gus trussed up like a hen. When the Cheyenne come along, find their gold gone and no guns, I reckon they'll take it out on Pa and finish him for us."

"My way's a sure thing. And I won't be wondering," Zack said, opening the front door an inch wider after a gust of wind had closed the crack.

"But it can get you hanged!"

Zack's head snapped around and his eyes turned hard. "Who's to tell?"

Jay Lee blanched, his piggish features whitening as he tried to make light of his remarks. "Have it your way." He shrugged. Now was a time for action, for force of arms. Later there would be a need for clever planning. Jay Lee had faith in his own cunning. Zack only knew one way to handle things, with violence. Jay Lee considered himself to be a man of intelligence. And men of intelligence would inherit the earth.

Still, he did not enjoy being shamed in front of Becca, a woman whose physical charms had also captivated him. Thoughts of her filled his nights with illicit dreams and troubled sleep.

"So be it," Jay Lee sighed. Despite the cold air rushing in through the gap in the partly opened doorway, perspiration beaded the fat man's brow. He patted his whispy hair and smoothed it flat.

Becca Hammond pressed herself against Zack, and ran her hand along his arm and then along the rifle barrel. The buffalo gun seemed to possess its own peculiar and sentient aura of death. The gun's heavy, solid construction boosted her confidence. She lifted her gaze toward the barn's open doorway and silently willed her husband to show himself.

Black smoke drifted from the tin stack on the barn's roof. Gus was still working his forge, she imagined. He had been shaping an iron rim for a new wagon wheel.

"Damn, how long can it take?" Becca swore, her pale cheeks flushed, her eyes as dark as her heart.

Zack was as impatient as the woman beside him. For almost a year now he had watched and waited, his desire burning within like a fever that threatened to consume him.

A father and two sons, three men alone in the heart of the howling wilderness and Becca Hammond the only white woman in these lonely mountains. Zack felt no fealty toward his father. The trader had never shown his sons affection.

"He's treated me and Jay Lee more like indentured servants than his own flesh and blood," Zack muttered.

"But today it all comes home," Becca said and ran her pink tongue over her lips, her gaze held an open invitation. "You'll have me *and* his gold." She looked through the doorway, her hands opening and closing. For a long moment no one said anything; the silence spoke volumes for them.

At last it was Jay Lee who shattered the tableau and headed for the door.

"What're you fixin' to do?" Zack asked.

"End this," Jay Lee replied. He brushed the Sharps aside and strode out through the door. Watery rolls of fat jostled beneath his shirt as he trotted the forty or so yards to the barn doorway. He took a moment to catch his breath and looked over his shoulder at the tracks in the snow stretching back toward the house. He gulped the cold air into his lungs and returned his attention to the barn. "Now we'll see who's a man of action."

At the edge of the forest just past the barn, a rabbit scampered across the cleared ground and darted toward the line of trees that bordered a trail leading to a spring. The shadow of a hawk skimmed soundlessly over the landscape. The play of hunter and hunted was not lost on Jay Lee, who glimpsed his own role in the order of things. He did not relish being a decoy, but he could no longer endure the waiting.

"What the hell are you up to, back so soon?" Gus's

gruff voice bellowed from the shadowy recesses of the
barn. The ring of a hammer beating iron pealed on an
icy north breeze. Jay Lee shivered and wished he had
worn his coat.

"We didn't check the traps," he called out.

"Why the hell not?"

"We came across somethin' you oughta take a look
at."

"Injun sign? If them red devils show up and I ain't
got their guns yet from the Landing, the fat'll be in
the fire for sure," Gus said, appearing just inside the
door. He wore a red flannel shirt, Levis, and a coarse
leather apron, and carried a short-handled smithy's
hammer in his hand. Gus was a squat, thickly muscled
man with weathered skin and oily brown hair, whose
features were soot-streaked and set in a perpetual
scowl.

"Maybe some Cheyenne, we can't tell." Lee
pointed toward the forest beyond the barn. "You ought
to check this for yourself, Pa."

"Tarnation! I taught you boys to read the signs,"
Gus said and spat a stream of tobacco on the packed
snow in front of the door. "I'm always having to do
for you and that worthless brother of yours." Gus
stepped into the sunlight and paused a couple of yards
in front of the doorway.

Now, Jay Lee silently said. *Now!* He waited and
Gus stared at him, somewhat perplexed by his son's
peculiar behavior.

"What the hell are you up to, fat boy?" Gus asked,

eyebrows arched as he studied the young man's face. "If this is some damn game . . . ?"

Lee swung around toward the house. "Now!" he sreamed.

The Sharps bellowed and a tongue of flame jetted from the barrel. Jay Lee flinched and tripped himself and sat down in the snow. He heard Gus Hammond loose a cry of pain and saw his father blown backward by the force of the bullet.

Hammond spun in midair, slammed against the wall of the barn, and dropped to the ground, where he began an ungainly crawl toward the doorway.

A crawl? He wasn't dead. Jay Lee bolted upright and scrambled to his feet, dusting the snow from his shirt and wool trousers.

"Sonuvabitch," Gus groaned as he pulled himself along. His left arm dangled uselessly; a gaping hole spewed blood from his shattered shoulder and collarbone. His right hand snaked out and he dragged himself forward another couple of inches. He had a revolver just inside the door if only he could reach it. Suddenly he stood and stumbled into the barn.

"You missed, you damn fool!" Jay Lee shouted toward the house, where Zack was frantically reloading. Jay Lee took the initiative and hurried toward the doorway as Gus lurched into the shadows. He grabbed the hammer Gus had dropped and followed his father out of the light. He could barely see, as his eyes adjusted to the dimly lit interior, Gus Hammond reaching up toward a holstered revolver. The older man was on his knees and the gun dangled from a peg just out of reach. His shaking fingers stretched toward the gun grip.

With a quickness that defied his hefty size, Jay Lee crossed the distance to his father's side and, arm raised, brought the hammer down in a brutal arc. The iron mallet caved in the back of Gus Hammond's skull with a sickening crunch of bone, killing him instantly and dropping him to the straw-littered floor.

Jay Lee staggered back a step, let the hammer slip from his grasp, and then walked wearily from the barn. "It's done," he shouted as he emerged into the cold sunlight and saw Zak, rifle in hand, standing on the porch. Becca stood alongside, obviously worried. "He's dead."

Zack cheered and fired the buffalo gun into the air. He set the rifle aside and scooped Becca up in his arms and hurried inside to claim his reward. By the time Jay Lee reached the house, climbed the steps to the front door, and entered the house Zack had already taken Becca to the dead man's bed.

Jay Lee waited a moment and listened to the sounds of lovemaking that drifted in through the closed door.

"The blood isn't even dry yet," he muttered. And his mind was filled with black conjecture and bitter thoughts. He continued into the kitchen, where three sacks of gold dust had been set in the center of the broad oaken table that dominated the center of the room. There was coffee on the cookstove, but he moved to the pantry and found a jug of his father's uncut corn whiskey, meant for personal consumption.

Gus had always cut his injun whiskey with water and sometimes a little fermented honey.

"We ain't got time for dallying," he shouted, hoping to talk sense into Zack. He received no response. Jay Lee uncorked the jug and drank deeply, letting the fiery liquid burn his gullet and warm him to his toes. He listened enviously to the moans of pleasure emanating from the bedroom. He tilted the jug to his lips yet again and then grabbed up one of the pouches of gold dust and stuffed it into his pocket. He found a coat hanging from a wall rack and pulled it on.

If Zack wanted to roll in the bed with Becca, so be it. But Jay Lee Hammond was getting the hell out. He loathed the idea of having to reenter the barn, but that's where the horses were kept. Nothing to be done about it and, anyway, Gus Hammond was dead. The smart thing to do was move out and be quick before the Cheyenne arrived for rifles that weren't even here.

In the front room, Jay Lee slung a saddlebag of provisions off the back of a chair and helped himself to the Henry rifle from the wall rack over the hearth. He patted the pouch of gold dust to reassure himself he still had it, then started toward the front door. He hesitated once, considering whether or not he should announce his departure.

"The hell with it," he muttered and threw open the front door. And froze in his tracks.

Raven and High-Backed Wolf and a war party of Red Shield Cheyenne were arranged on horseback in a line blocking Jay Lee's route of escape.

Raven, wearing a necklace of two-day-old scalps,

lowered the cruel-looking tip of his spear and pointed toward the Henry rifle still in Jay Lee's grasp. His blood-red visage remained unfathomable, but when he spoke, his tone was ripe with menace and disdain.

"We have come for our guns," he said.

6

★

It had been three long days of wearying ascents back-tracking, and paralleling the main trail to Hammond's place. Another war party had been spotted, forcing Cole, Sergeant McKane, and Ben Wheatley to lie low and keep to cover. The weather itself held clear and cold despite the advent of spring. The ground wore an icy carpet of snow that slowed the men's pace and made it impossible to travel without leaving a set of tracks that marked their passage.

They had slept fitfully at best, for a fire was out of the question. The crackers and jerked beef lasted a day and a half. After that it was tight belts and empty bellies.

At last, on the afternoon of the third day, the three climbed a long slope, overlooking Hammond's trading post.

"The Northern Rockies, my lads," McKane said with a wave of his hand towards the purple peaks that rose far beyond the small valley. "Call it the High Lonesome if your skin is white." His breath came in wheezing gasps as he trailed the two younger men up the steep ridge.

"Or the Backbone of the World if it's red." Cole grinned from the crest of the incline. He offered the gray-haired Irishman a hand up, which the sergeant gratefully accepted as he scrambled to the top.

"Or Hell on Heels if your skin is black," Ben Wheatley said and settled on a perch of granite. He yanked off a worn boot and began massaging his right foot. He sighed, enjoying the respite. All three men studied the trading post below.

Gus Hammond had chosen the location of his homestead wisely, hiding his house and barn in a narrow valley that cut through the cliffs. The cabin was a long log building with a steeply pitched roof. The barn was a two-storied structure built from lumbered pine and twice as large as the cabin.

From their vantage point, the trading post seemed devoid of life. Cole didn't like the premonition he was feeling.

"There's always someone about," McKane whispered. "Either Gus or one of his boys. He's a man with little trust in the honesty of his fellow man and never leaves the place without someone to watch over things."

Cole cradled the Winchester '66 in the crook of his arm and studied the clearing until he had decided on the route he would take down to the cabin.

"You want me to check it out?" McKane asked, scratching his gray head.

Cole looked at him. "You trying to be nice, Sergeant?"

"Well, you know what they say," the soldier chuckled and fished a plug of tobacco out of his greatcoat. "Age before beauty." He bit a chewful of tobacco.

"You figure our Cheyenne friends might be down there, Cole?" Ben asked. He eyed the homesite with suspicion.

"Only one way to find out," Cole said.

"Wheatley and me'll cover you," McKane offered.

"I hoped you might," Cole answered, checking the action of his carbine. "If Medicine Bear and his braves are down there, I'd appreciate you making every shot count for something."

McKane nodded and descended to a stand of timber several yards below. Wheatley took up a position alongside the sergeant.

Cole paused as he drew abreast of the two men. He nodded to McKane, who patted the Springfield nestled in his grasp. Cole continued on, keeping to a game trail that curved down the slope. Here and there, barren slabs of granite poked through the snow to form a scene desolate in the gray light of the feeble sun.

And ominous in its silence.

Back on the ridge, Wheatley and McKane studied Anthem's cautious, winding descent. Cole glided catlike among the trees. As they watched, Wheatley heard the sergeant mutter, "Mark me, that lad's more'n a wrangler. I guessed it to look at him. Seen him during the fight at the wagons. He's breathed his share of powder smoke."

* * *

Cole emerged from the edge of the woods and started across the broad yard to the house. He approached it head on, moving straight toward the porch. Every few seconds he glanced over his shoulder at the barn. He almost wished for a war whoop, a cry of rage, and a swarm of Red Shields. Anything to break the grim, silent tableau he had entered. But nothing happened. He heard only the wind's steady moan, barely audible as it swept across the valley and stirred the branches of the lodgepole pines. With a last crouching dash Cole reached the porch, climbed the stairs in a single bound, and flattened himself against the outside wall.

And still the silence held, broken by nothing more than an intermittent drip of water that spilled from the corner of the roof and landed in a small puddle in front of him.

A glint from the hill caught his eye. Cole could make out the huddled forms of the two men whose rifles were trained on the house and barn. McKane was an experienced hand. But if trouble came, young Wheatley might just as easily wind up shooting Anthem as an Indian. The notion offered little comfort.

Drawing a deep breath, Cole ducked under a window and moved to the corner of the house, peered around, and saw nothing to alert him. He eased back to his position by the front. The snow-covered yard had been trampled and churned by what appeared to have been several unshod ponies.

Cheyenne. But where were they now? Across the yard, the barn stood with its big doors hanging open.

The black, empty doorway was menacing.

Cole reached for the latch on the cabin door. Swinging open at the slight pressure from his hand, the plank door groaned and creaked on its iron hinges and, in the silence, sounded louder than it actually was.

Cole paused to allow his vision to adjust. He thumbed the hammer back on his Winchester and waited. And once again, nothing. Only a couple of overturned chairs. Another couple of ladderbacks appeared not to have been disturbed in the corner. Underfoot, a bearskin was smeared with mud and stank of whiskey. On the wall were the bolts from a rifle rack that had been yanked down and emptied.

Cole crossed quickly to the partially open door leading to a room to the left of the front living area. He knew what he would find.

Redhaired Becca Hammond lay across the bed, her head bent back over the edge of it. She greeted him upside-down with a wide-eyed empty gaze. Her mouth hung open as if frozen in a scream. Her dark and grotesquely swollen tongue protruded from between her teeth. The bruised, discolored skin of her throat showed she had been strangled. Her naked body bore other marks as well, and Cole had no doubt she had been raped repeatedly before being killed. Death must have come as a friend.

Cole walked to the bedside and covered the woman's naked form with a coarse sheet that reeked of whiskey. On the floor at the foot of the bed were the remains of her flannel shirt and trousers. A dresser had been overturned and its contents strewn over the floor on the opposite side of the bed.

A dull ache pounded in Cole's head as he stared grimly at the distorted, pitiful figure before him. He suppressed his emotions, fearing they might lead him to rash action. Rashness was a death sentence in the bounty hunter's trade.

Death was no stranger to him. And yet, for all his efforts he had failed to become immune to that grim and inevitable finality. Too many people had fallen to Medicine Bear's brutal Red Shields. It was time the braves were held accountable. Cole looked down at the useless weapon in his grasp. There was no one to kill, no one to answer for these bloody deeds. But there would be. There would be. . . .

"The old man's dead in the barn."

Cole swiveled about in a crouch, his finger tightening on the trigger of his carbine as he brought the Yellowboy to bear on the man who had crept up behind him. Cole's expression changed from an animal snarl to a look of surprise. He eased off the trigger, a fraction of a second away from putting a bullet through Sam Dollard.

Dollard smiled, showing a crooked line of yellow teeth, and stepped into the bedroom. He held his Henry rifle in his left hand, away from his body. The right hand was raised, palm up. "Easy, Cole. I ain't wearin' no war paints."

Sam Dollard was a solidly built, short man, thick featured with black bushy eyebrows and ferret eyes that always seemed to be searching and rarely stopped to meet a man's stare. A much chewed-on cigar dangled from his mouth. He looked past Cole at the body of Becca Hammond. "She's a mess, ain't she. You reckon she's too cold to dip into?"

Cole's fist crashed against the scout's unprotected mouth. Dollard didn't see it coming. He flew backward and landed on the bearskin rug in the front room. Somehow he managed to hang on to his Henry rifle, which he used to prop himself up on his knees.

"Get up, you bastard. There's more coming. Stand up and take it," Cole said.

Dollard wiped the back of his hand across his bloodied mouth. Slowly he shook his head and tried to clear his blurred vision. "Are you loco or somethin', Anthem?" he slurred.

"Stand up."

Dollard lunged forward, swinging the Henry like a club. That was one mistake. Missing was another. Cole hit him again. He caught the scout along the jaw and throat with another vicious right that sent Dollard hurtling out the front door, knocking one of the hinges loose.

Dollard landed hard in the front yard, the rifle spinning from his grasp. He spit snow from his mouth and felt the world turning black. He maintained consciousness and forced himself to action. He reached for the Henry repeater and saw the Texan on the porch aim with his Winchester. Dollard sucked wind to cry out for help.

"No use in that. I'm the only one here," Cole said. "The whole detail you were supposed to be scouting for is gone. You killed them, Sam, sure as I'm standing here, sure as you're lying there ready to join them."

Dollard trembled. The Henry was out of reach. The crazy bastard was going to kill him. Confused, the scout tried to crawl away from the deadly muzzle aimed at his heart. "I couldn't help it," he wailed through a mouthful of blood.

He must have said the wrong thing again, for suddenly Cole came down from the porch, caught the scout by the scruff of his shirt, and dragged him to his feet.

"Where were you, you bastard?"

Blood streamed from Dollard's puffed lips as he struggled for air. A thin red line trickled down his chin onto the iron hand clenched closely under his chin. Cole's hard blue eyes bore into the scout's, and he seemed far older than his twenty-four years.

"Medicine Bear got between me and the camp. It was all I could do to keep those Red Shields from findin' me," Dollard exclaimed, struggling to convince Cole of his good intentions. His words came rapidly, revealing his fear. "I knew it would be bad, but what else was I gonna do? I lost my horse and everything!"

Slowly Cole's other hand brought the business end of the carbine up beneath Dollard's chin. The scout didn't breathe, he didn't even dare swallow. At last Cole replied quietly, in a venomous tone. All he said was a single word. "Later."

Dollard shuddered and stumbled back as Cole released him and walked toward the barn. The scout sighed and gratefully began to gasp for fresh air.

"I seen you from the barn," Dollard said. "I stayed hid till I recognized who it was. You'll find Gus in the barn." He wiped his split lip across his sleeve and reached for the Henry. For a moment he considered evening the score, then reconsidered. He was still too wobbly from the beating to chance a shot. And he knew the first one would have to count.

On his way to the barn, Cole looked up toward the ridge and spied McKane and Wheatley hurrying down the slope. He motioned for them to join him and then continued toward the barn.

The anger in Cole was slow to subside and only gradually did the intensity lessen in his eyes.

Gus Hammond lay facedown on the straw-covered floor. His outstretched arms seemed to be groping for something. The blood had dried and turned black. Flies buzzed around the gaping bullet wound to his shoulder and caved-in skull. A black-stained hammer lay on the ground a few feet away. Anthem frowned and walked closer to inspect the hammer. Bits of bone as well as a fragment of matted hair were stuck to the head of the mallet. The shock of the blow had clearly turned the brains to jelly inside the smashed skull. Gus Hammond must have died immediately, Cole speculated.

Dollard's voice jolted Anthem back to the present. "Cheyenne been here." The scout lounged in the doorway; a languid hand gestured toward the gloomy interior of the barn. "Stole all the horses, too, the murdering thieves."

Anthem surveyed the empty stalls. Smoke still rose from the embers of the forge.

"Found this, too," Dollard said. He tossed a broken arrow shaft to the ground at Anthem's foot.

The arrow was Cheyenne, all right. Medicine Bear's Red Shields had been through here. Slowly Cole turned again to look at Hammond. But something was wrong. Why kill the man with a hammer? Why kill him at all, for that matter. Wasn't Hammond a friend to the Cheyenne?

And he had also been shot with a buffalo gun. An Indian might have one, true. But weren't Hammond and his sons buffalo hunters? And where were his sons?

"Mother of mercy, if it ain't Sam Dollard," Sergeant Danny McKane said from the doorway. "So it was you the Texan was poundin'. If ever a man deserved it." The sergeant continued on into the barn. "And that's Gus Hammond?!"

"He's dead!" Wheatley said, drawing up with the Irishman to see what was going on. He saw and wished he hadn't.

"Dead? Yeah, there's a lot of it going around," Cole replied, tossing the broken arrow aside. "Don't know who will be next." He looked at Dollard. "We can rest up here tonight and move on tomorrow," he added. He stepped between Wheatley and the sergeant out through the open doorway.

Ben Wheatley, his stomach turning, shook his head and added in a woeful voice, "It's gonna be a long night."

7

★

The clouds had parted enough by the end of the day to allow a ribbon of pink and royal purple light to streak the western horizon. Shadows stole across the forested hillsides and masked the valleys, making passage all but impossible for the unfamiliar.

An hour's ride from their father's homestead, Zack and Jay Lee Hammond slowed their winded mounts to a walk.

"You reckon we lost them," Jay Lee said, calling in a whisper to his brother.

"Hell yes," came the reply as Zack ducked a low-hanging branch of aspen and paused to get his bearings. "Them red devils would never suspect us of backtracking to Pa's."

"Yeah, they don't reckon us to be such fools."

"We're alive, ain't we?" Zack retorted. "Hell, Jay Lee, if you're so damn trail-wise, why don't you take the lead?"

"I didn't mean nothing," Jay Lee said, hoping to soothe his brother's injured pride.

"Well, if'n you don't mean nothing then shut the hell up!" Zack wiped a forearm across his features. He'd ridden home this way before. He knew the lay of the land, but still it did not hurt to be careful. He eyed the surrounding forest. Every quaking branch of rustling bush seemed cause for alarm. Zack wished desperately for a gun.

"Zack, where are you?" Jay Lee called, a note of panic in his voice.

"Here, damn it, and better lower your voice," the younger brother said, walking his horse away from the aspen. Jay Lee was too easily spooked and was about as useful as a dry well when it came to it. But it had been Jay Lee who had persuaded the Cheyenne to let the brothers set off for Morgan's Landing to get the rifles. Of course, the Hammonds had no intention of ever facing a Red Shield again. The ruse had kept them alive, no doubt about it. So Jay Lee had his uses and Zack was willing to put up with his older brother's faults. At least for the time being.

The horses plodded through the snowy landscape, steam jetting from their flared nostrils, lather freezing on their necks and flanks. The brothers rode in silence now, each in his own way dealing with the dismal turn of events. Everything was lost, the guns, the gold, and redhaired Becca Hammond. They didn't even have a saddle between them. Nothing but the clothes on their backs and a pair of winded mounts.

Jay Lee's stomach growled. He winced at the pangs of hunger and wished he could sit down to a plate of antelope steaks and pan gravy. Plate, hell, a whole damn platter.

"You reckon High-Backed Wolf or Raven left anything in the root cellar?" Jay Lee asked. "Even salt meat and beans'd go good right now."

"You better quit worryin' about your belly and start worryin' about your scalp," Zack hissed. He spoke in a harsh whisper. "Now, I told you to ride quiet. Sound carries hereabouts and it won't do to announce ourselves."

We ought to be clear by now, Jay Lee thought. As many as there were of those savages we'd hear them come up on us. In the distance the mournful cry of a lobo wolf rang across the land. *It must be the loneliest sound in the world. That is, if it is a wolf.* The older brother began to search the night, his fear building. He felt a vise tightening about his throat, slowly strangling him. And he kept repeating in his mind there was nothing to be afraid of. Zack was right. The war party would surely expect them to ride toward the Rogue and the outpost under construction nearby. So he and Zack were safe and had nothing to worry about but salvaging what they could from the homestead, then fleeing for Fort Conrad.

The more Jay Lee reasoned and watched Zack unerringly guide them homeward, the more his fears eased. For the first time he began to feel safe. Ahead, Jay Lee noticed his brother round a thick cluster of lodgepole pines and vanish from sight. Jay Lee gulped nervously and tried to make his recalcitrant mount close ranks with the animal ahead. The Indian pony

refused to even try. A stubborn mare, it endured Jay
Lee's muttered curses and rounded the stand at its own
tired pace.

Zack's horse, riderless now, waited a few yards
ahead. Jay Lee's blood turned to ice in his veins, and
he drove his booted heels against the mare in a burst
of savage kicks. The mare, fed up with the fat man's
tactics, reared and pawed the air, dumping him uncer-
emoniously on a carpet of pine needles.

The older Hammond rolled onto his knees, gasped
for breath, and listened to the laughter emanating from
the shadows. He could barely make out Zack's inert
form, the shallow rise and fall of his chest.

Someone moved on the fringes of the night, the
someone who continued to laugh.

"Oh, my God," Jay Lee whimpered.

The warrior called Raven materialized out of the
dark. He held a stone war club in one hand, a whiskey
jug in his right. He looked drunk. And mean. Raven
began to laugh as he advanced on the terror-riveted
man.

Jay Lee screamed. The sound of his voice mingled
with that of the wolf's distant cry.

The embers of the fire crackled, spiraling upward
through the stone chimney. Cole Anthem turned his
back on the hearth and the three men asleep on the
floor, and ambled out onto the porch to be alone with
the darkness, the silence, and his own thoughts.

It had taken more than an hour to hack a pair of
graves in the frozen earth. Dollard had kept up a

stream of complaints but to no avail. Over the years Cole Anthem had left too many bodies for the wolves. He was determined now to see Gus and Becca decently buried. Sergeant McKane, meanwhile, had prepared a meal of beans and bacon from a supply of goods the Red Shields have overlooked.

A decision had been reached to continue on to Morgan's Landing in hopes of encountering Major Busby's command along the way. The major was a bullnecked, determined little man, eager to fulfill his orders to build a new military outpost right in the heart of the mountain country, the better to maintain a military presence among the savages. A devout Calvinist, the major saw it as his appointed mission to bring civilization to the Cheyenne and Blackfoot tribes.

Cole sat on the corner of the porch, his Winchester balanced on his lap, and he replayed the events of the afternoon in his mind's eye.

The wood flooring creaked and Cole glanced aside as Ben Wheatley hesitated in the doorway, unsure whether or not he should disturb Anthem. But Cole motioned for him to come on.

"You make a good target with the firelight at your back," Cole said.

Ben shoved his hands in the pockets of his overcoat and joined the bounty hunter on the porch. He looked out at the twin crosses rising out of the dirty white snow.

" 'What a piece of work is a man, how noble in reason, how infinite in faculties,' " Wheatley quoted, his bass voice soft yet resonant, " 'In form and moving how express and admirable, in action how like an angel, in apprehension how like a god.' " He faltered, his memory failing, then he concluded. " 'And yet to me, what is this quintessence of dust?' " He nodded, satisfied, then looked at Cole. "That's Shakespeare. *Hamlet.* Doc Fleming had a fine library. And I worked my way from one bookend to the other." Wheatley sighed. "I amused his friends to no end because I was more than what I appeared to be." He looked at Cole. "So are you, at least that's what McKane thinks. He says that Cole Anthem is a sight more than a wrangler. 'If anybody can get us out of this fix, it's Anthem.' "

"McKane can gab, all right," Cole replied. "Never met an Irishman who couldn't."

"But he's correct, is he not?"

"Words don't count for much out here, Ben," Cole said. "It's what a man does." He removed his hat and brushed his sun-bleached hair back with a sweep of his big broad hand. "Yeah, I've done a few other things in my time. Hell, I can't be more than a few years older than you."

"I know Shakespeare. But you know how to stay alive," Ben said ruefully. "I get your meaning." He crooked his thumb toward the doorway, the merest hint of a smile upon his face. A muscle twitched along his prominent cheekbone. "It appears you have no use for the likes of Mr. Dollard." The scout had spoken no more than a few curt orders to Ben throughout the day, making it obvious he considered the black man nothing more than a servant.

"Oh, I have a use for Sam Dollard," Cole soberly

replied. He stiffened suddenly, his grip tightening on the Winchester. He listened, intensity in his features, his long lanky frame poised to move. He searched the night and found at last the source of the noise that had alerted him.

A big gray wolf skirted the perimeter of trees, its paw pads crunching the snow. The predator had caught the scent of blood and come searching for a carcass to drag back to its den. It froze in midstep and noticed for the first time the two men on the porch. The wolf raised its head, nostrils flared as it identified the human scent. Then it retreated toward the forest and vanished among the timber.

Cole relaxed.

Ben, his educated mind filled with the fantasy of an impending Indian attack, whistled lowly as he exhaled. He looked down at his hands. They were trembling. He hoped Cole hadn't noticed.

"Better get your rifle," Cole said. "Then you'll have something to cling to. It works all right for me."

The black man studied Anthem, unable to believe he had anything but melted ice in his veins. Cole patted the Winchester lying across his lap to emphasize the truth of his advice.

"Don't see what good a rifle will do." Wheatley scoffed and moved forward to stand in the snowy yard a few feet from Cole. "I hid out in that beaver pond and didn't fire a single shot. I have never killed a man. Never taken a human life." He wiped his face and blew his nose in a kerchief. "It is not an easy thing to even contemplate."

"I hope it never gets to be," Cole said. "See here, Ben. Back in Boston maybe the meek will inherit the earth but out here west of the Mississippi, all they get is six feet of dirt. That's if someone's kind enough to plant them."

"I've been wondering . . . maybe I'm a coward," Wheatley muttered. He turned and mounted the porch steps.

Cole called, "Wheatley . . ."

The black man halted, waiting, his hand on the door latch.

"When trouble comes, I think you'll stand with us," the bounty hunter said, and hoped he sounded confident enough for the both of them.

Sam Dollard rolled out of his bedroll and grumbled at the man who had awakened him. He made a surreptitious check of his few belongings, for he trusted no one, and then sat back on his haunches, rubbing the sleep out of his eyes and wincing at the still tender lip where Cole's fists had marked him.

"Something the matter?" he grumbled, looking up at Sergeant McKane.

McKane jabbed a thumb toward Cole and Wheatley, who were already taking their coffee by the fire. There wasn't much left in the root cellar, but to a hungry man, coffee, beans, and stale biscuits was a feast.

"Time we got goin', laddiebuck," the sergeant said.

"We gonna walk to Morgan's Landing?" Dollard asked, fatigue already in his voice.

The sergeant straightened, brushed the dust from his faded blue army-issue trousers, and then looked to either side as if he expected someone to eavesdrop. "Well, no Sam," he answered. "I thought we might hitch us a ride on the Wednesday stage. It should be through here any minute now."

"My feet hear you talkin', McKane," Dollard sourly retorted. "Too bad they ain't in a humorous mood, just like the rest of me."

"Just so you keep up with us, Dollard. That's all you have to do," Cole said from near the fire.

"I'll go where I please. And no goddamn wrangler is gonna tell me otherwise."

The room grew quiet. Ben Wheatley stared down at the steaming contents of his cup and tried to decide which was thicker, the silence or the coffee. Opposite him, Cole slowly stood.

"That's fine, Dollard. Pick your trail and go on. But the Henry and your belly gun stay with us," Anthem said. His right arm hung loose at his side, his hand dangling just below the handle of his Colt. Eyes like chipped ice, blue and cold as the very heart of a norther, never wavered and held a promise of death.

What the hell kind of wrangler was this? Dollard wondered. He appraised Anthem anew, realizing he knew nothing of the Texan. He had only occasionally encountered Cole at Fort Conrad, and exchanged nothing more than pleasantries and camp talk throughout Fleming's survey expedition. Dollard could see now that Anthem was someone to step around.

"Hell, I reckon I'll tag along, seein' as you feel so

strongly on the matter," Dollard said with a shrug that defused the situation. He ran a forearm over his mouth, licked his dry lips, and inhaled the strong scent of coffee. "Say, boy, bring me a cup of that." His gaze fixed on Wheatley. "Hey, are you deaf or what?"

Cole started to speak up and then thought better of it.

"Did you hear me, boy? You were Doc Fleming's nigger, weren't you? I'll take some coffee."

Wheatley looked up at Cole expectantly. At first the black man frowned angrily when Cole didn't come to his defense. *And I took him for a friend*, Wheatley thought. *The devil take Cole Anthem and Sam Dollard.*

"Get your own damn coffee," he snapped and, turning his back on the men in the room, he stalked off through the front door.

"What's eating him?" Dollard asked, his bushy brows arched and a look of innocence plain for all to see. "Did you see that? I damn near get my balls shot off at Gettysburg fighting for his kind, and I can't even get a cup of coffee from the little pickaninny." He wagged his head as he decried the changing world. "Maybe we should have let you Johnny Rebs win," he added for Cole's benefit. But Anthem didn't pay him any mind and left by the front door, taking up his Winchester before stepping outside.

Cole found Wheatley leaning against a corner post, watching the crimson blush of sunrise tinge the eastern sky. The bounty hunter cleared his throat to announce himself. He hooked a thumb in his gunbelt, cradled the Yellowboy in the crook of his arm.

"You know," Cole said, "out here a man's got to show he can stand before he can expect others to stand with him."

Wheatley nodded, reflecting on Anthem's statement. His facial expression betrayed his anger. "Tell me, Anthem, you ever get sick of hearing yourself talk?" he asked.

"All the time," Cole chuckled, taking no offense.

Wheatley couldn't help himself and grinned at last, amused by the Texan's lack of seriousness about himself. Ben wondered just what chance Cole would have stood if Dollard had called him out. Eyeing the brass-framed Winchester '66, Ben asked, "Are you really any good with that?"

"I can make it dance," Cole replied, with nary a trace of humor in his voice now. Some things a man just didn't make light of. Wheatley started to offer a response, but Cole hushed him and stepped to the edge of the porch.

He heard it again, the sound unmistakable. Gunfire echoed down the long hills. Not enough to suggest a pitched battle but oddly spaced shots, all the more puzzling and disconcerting for their infrequency.

McKane appeared on the front porch and, shading his eyes, studied the northernmost ridge as he listened. "Who do you reckon it is?"

"Only one way to know for sure," Cole replied.

"Yeah," McKane agreed with a sigh. And ruefully added, "I was afraid you were gonna say that."

8

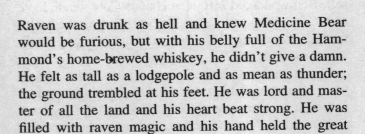

Raven was drunk as hell and knew Medicine Bear would be furious, but with his belly full of the Hammond's home-brewed whiskey, he didn't give a damn. He felt as tall as a lodgepole and as mean as thunder; the ground trembled at his feet. He was lord and master of all the land and his heart beat strong. He was filled with raven magic and his hand held the great mystery of life and death.

He extended his right arm, squinted, squeezed the trigger. The Colt revolver bucked in his hand, and a bullet whined past Jay Lee Hammond's right ear.

The fat man was tied upright and spread-eagled between two aspens. He pulled against the leather cords encircling his wrists and ankles and screamed for Zack to help him.

Brother Zack had troubles of his own, however. He lay near the smoldering embers of last night's campfire and watched his brother strain and twist. Zack's hands were bound behind his back while another length of leather tightly circled his ankles and calves.

A Cheyenne brave sat across from him, watching and now and then taking a pull from a jug of whiskey and grinning at him.

There was no mercy on the warrior's scarred face, only a blurred look of anticipation as he emptied the dregs of the jug down his gullet, stood, and walked shakily over to Raven.

"Young Bull, give me your gun," Raven said, his speech slurred. "Gather more wood for the fire."

"Am I your squaw to be ordered about?" Young Bull retorted.

"If you were my squaw I would first crawl into my blanket with a buffalo." Raven laughed broadly while Young Bull glared with his one good eye. A livid length of scar tissue blazed his left cheek and scrawled upward to obliterate his left eye. His hand dropped to the elkhorn grip of the knife sheathed at his waist. He toyed with the idea of teaching Raven more respect for him. But even in his drunken state Young Bull couldn't ignore the Colt revolver Raven brandished or the second gun holstered at his side.

So Young Bull sucked in a chestful of clear, cold mountain air and stumbled off to do as he was told. He hoped Raven would soon have his fill of the white men. Now that the whiskey was gone, Young Bull was eager to rejoin High-Backed Wolf and the others who had gone to the river. There was no powerful medicine to be gained from torturing the likes of the Hammonds. Their hearts were like rabbits'. They were not men of courage.

Twenty yards into the woods, Young Bull was

brought up sharply. What was that he had heard, a cracking branch? He stood still in the shadow of the pines and tried to listen. Maybe it was too much whiskey. His brain labored to decipher what had made the noise, or was there a noise? In the clearing, Raven sighted down the barrel of the Colt, squeezed the trigger, and blew off the tip of Jay Lee Hammond's left ear.

Anthem turned to glare at Dollard, who shrugged and lifted his foot off the brittle branch he had stepped on. The scout spat a stream of tobacco into the snow and placed his foot back into the trail left by Anthem. Off to the left, on the other side of a grove of saplings, Sergeant McKane raised a hand to signal Ben Wheatley to stop. A gunshot followed by a shriek of pain reverberated down the hillside.

Cole tried to judge the distance but sounds could be deceiving in mountain country. He motioned for Dollard to swing over to the right and close the gap with Wheatley and McKane. Cole did not relish having the scout directly at his back. He wanted to be able to watch the man. Though Dollard, for all his dislike of Anthem, seemed willing to put his animosity aside and recognize that Medicine Bear and the Red Shields were the most immediate threat, Cole felt like a target. He made sure the scout continued to weave his way up through the trees.

The sun was directly overhead. The stand of lodgepole pines grew thick here: saplings struggling for their share of sunlight filled the gaps among the larger trees and made progress not only difficult but also treacherous, for every shadow rising in the emerald gloom might well be a Cheyenne warrior leaping to the attack.

Wheatley tried to hide his nervousness. He concentrated on carefully placing his feet and on the weight of the breechloader he carried. He glanced aside, reassuring himself of the sergeant's presence.

"Looks like we're about to buy ourselves some trouble," the black man softly muttered.

"Buy, hell. It's free. Only this time you ain't gonna be watchin' from a distance, Ben," the sergeant answered with a grin.

Wheatley gave the man a hard look. "As I remember, McKane, we hid out together." He fished in his coat pocket for his cartridges, suddenly worried he had lost his ammunition. He fumbled with a handful and two or three precious rounds dropped into the soggy snow.

"Take it easy, Wheatley," McKane directed. "We got time yet. Bad enough that these here Springfields hold only one shell at a time without you losin' all your extras. And clean 'em off, mind you, for I'd not be wanting your gun to jam when the game gets hot."

Wheatley's head bobbed quickly in compliance, and he retrieved the shells and wiped them clean on his coat. "What if there's as many Cheyenne as at the wagon fight, Sergeant?" Ben asked, his voice a strained whisper.

"Why, we'll just find us a nice cozy little creek to hide in, like we done there." McKane chuckled at his own wit, only to be cut off by another high-pitched scream ahead. A deathly silence fell over the men. A gunshot sounded, followed by yet another scream. The voice was clear, obviously that of a white man. "Please, oh Jesus, oh-hhh-ooo," it called, the vowel drawn out and rising at the end to a thin, terror-stricken screech. Another voice called out, "Take it like a man, Jay Lee. Show him the Hammonds is men."

Wheatley listened in horror, his blood turning cold in his veins. He gave a start as a form materialized at his elbow. Cole waved to them both.

"Hurry along," Cole whispered. "And don't fire until we know what we're buying into."

The bounty hunter bolted off at a trot, his boots crunching in the snow as he leaped over fallen timber and outcroppings of snow-sprinkled granite.

Ben managed to keep up with Cole. The young black man was smaller but able to match Anthem's lengthy stride with his own darting quickness. As for Danny McKane, he gradually fell behind, aged muscles and the lay of the land taking their toll.

Cole was in his element now, and every sense became attuned to the world around him. He was the hunted no longer but the hunter. And it wasn't new to him. Some men built railroads, some drove stages, some soldiered, some mined, some farmed or built empires, like John Anthem, his father. Cole hunted men. And he did it better than most, coldly, methodically, and, most important of all, patiently.

He rounded a thicket of pine saplings, the trees no

bigger in diameter than a closed fist, and halted in his tracks as if frozen in place. Ten yards up a deer trail a one-eyed Cheyenne brave broke a dead limb from a lightning-blasted tree. The crack of timber seemed deafening in the quiet. Branch in hand, Young Bull looked up. Sensing danger but unaware of Cole's presence, he pulled his knife. Behind him, Anthem repeated the gesture, drawing his own bone-handled blade, intending a silent kill so as not to alert any of the brave's companions.

A howling cry from Jay Lee Hammond pinpointed the location of the Cheyenne camp as another twenty or thirty yards beyond the one-eyed Indian. Cole palmed the knife in his right hand, cocked his arm. Then Ben stumbled into the clearing, coming face-to-face with the Cheyenne.

Young Bull stared for a moment in disbelief, a tableau that held but a second. Ben was just as surprised and snapped up his rifle at the sight of the knife-wielding Cheyenne.

"No," Cole rasped too late.

The black man panicked and fired his rifle. The Springfield thundered uselessly and Young Bull darted away as Ben fervishly dug another round from his pocket.

"Damn! Cole shouted and raced forward. He sheathed his knife, for the element of surprise was totally lost now. From his right Dollard's Henry rifle bellowed three times. Cole headed straight across the clearing, straight for the main camp. He had no intention of chasing the one-eyed brave and coming into

Sam Dollard's line of fire. Cole heard the Henry speak again, evidence that the scout was keeping the escaping brave entertained.

Cole skirted the campsite at a dead run and dove forward at the edge of the clearing as a Colt revolver roared. He slid on his belly as leaden death whispered in his ear and ricocheted back among the pines. Cole fired at a fleeting shape that darted toward the horses. It was a wasted shot. He turned his attention and counted four Indian ponies tethered fifty feet away. Cole sighted and shot apart the knot tying the tether rope to a tall straight pine. Two more well-placed shots into the ground sent the startled horses scampering out of reach. He didn't want any of the horses escaping to warn Medicine Bear.

Across the clearing, Raven changed his course and backtracked toward Jay Lee Hammond, still bound between two trees. Cole knew it was useless to try to hit the brave as he dashed between the trees. Reading the warrior's intentions, he levered off another four shots that severed the ropes binding the fat man's wrists and ankles.

"Run," Cole shouted.

But Jay Lee remained rooted in place, cradling his bloody left hand. Blood spilled from his ravaged ear. He merely staggered in a tight circle and moaned.

Zack rolled to the side of the clearing, hoping to place himself out of the line of fire. He yelled for someone to untie him and strained to free himself of his bonds.

A geyser of dirty snow erupted in Cole's face, momentarily blinding him. He twisted aside and another geyser spewed upward in the hollow his body had left in the snow. Raven emerged from the shadows, aimed his Colt at Anthem lying prone in the melting snow. **But when he squeezed the trigger, the hammer struck** an empty chamber. The Cheyenne tossed the gun aside and drew the Colt holstered at his thigh.

Cole's rifle spat flame. The Cheyenne spun, clutched his side, and staggered back toward Jay Lee, who watched in horror. He realized his danger but too late. Raven was upon him, grabbing Hammond and using him as a shield. The wicked gleam of a knife blade appeared beneath Jay Lee's throat, insuring that whichever direction Raven moved, the white man was sure to go.

"Somebody help me!" Jay Lee shouted, then thought better of it. "No! Don't shoot. Keep clear."

Ben entered the clearing and ducked as Raven swung his gun toward him. McKane arrived, puffing and wheezing from his exertions. He held his Springfield ready but was loathe to fire and endanger Hammond.

Raven alternated his aim, sighting first at Cole, then the black man, then the sergeant, and quickly back to Cole. He repeated the process, never lingering on one man long enough for the others to attempt anything. The warrior shouted at them.

Cole slowly stood and shouldered his rifle. "McKane, you speak his lingo better than me. Tell him to put down his gun and he won't be hurt."

"The hell you say," Zack interjected.

"Shut up," Cole said. There wasn't much to sight on. Jay Lee was heavyset enough to provide ample protection for the brave. Still, Cole could make out a portion of the Cheyenne's shoulder and neck. . . .

McKane translated Anthem's request in the warrior's own tongue. Raven started backing toward the thicket of trees to his rear. The horses had raced off in that general direction, so even wounded, the Red Shield still had a chance to escape. He shouted a lengthy retort back to the sergeant and continued his retreat.

"Well . . . ?" Cole asked, keeping his rifle trained on the patch of red-painted flesh just a couple of inches off to the side of Jay Lee's pale throat.

"I seen this buck before. They call him Raven. And it's a mean-natured lad he is, to be sure," McKane explained. "As for his sentiments . . . he's as cold as ice. Making it short and simple, let me put it this way, if you so much as blink he'll slit Hammond's throat from ear to ear."

McKane shifted his stance. Raven swung to bring him under the gun again. Cole never blinked and the carbine jumped in his grasp. The shot echoed as the bullet from the Yellowboy Winchester struck the side of the warrior's neck just above the collarbone, knocking him backward. Jay Lee crumpled to the ground, a hairline wound across his throat.

Raven, still standing, fired and missed. Cole fired and didn't.

Raven's head snapped back from the force of the slug; the brave toppled like felled timber and landed rump first in a drift. A pine at his back held him up-right in a sitting position, a blackened hole between his unseeing eyes.

Cole started across the clearing. He found a handful of shells in his coat pocket and immediately began loading the carbine.

"Holy shit," McKane said. It had all happened too fast for him to bring his Springfield into play.

Ben Wheatley knew he had blundered from the out-set. He stared down at his trembling hands and felt ashamed. He just hoped and prayed nobody mentioned his incompetence.

"Looks like I missed the fun," Sam Dollard said, stepping into the clearing from a deer trail off to Cole's right. "I had a party of my own," Dollard added with a grin and lifted a freshly taken Cheyenne scalp.

"Somebody cut me loose," Zack cried out in his fury.

"Oh God . . . oh God," Jay Lee continued to moan.

The sergeant knelt down by Zack and cut him free. Zack rolled to his feet, and charged past the campfire. Brushing past Cole, he headed straight for the dead brave propped upright against the trunk of the pine tree. There he retrieved his Colt, blew the snow from the barrel and cylinder.

"Red nigger son of a bitch!" Zack opened fire and emptied the gun into the corpse. It slid over on its side and still he continued to squeeze the trigger.

Click. Click. Click.

Cole reached Zack and snatched the gun from his grasp. As he turned on the man who had saved him,

Zack Hammond's features were contorted in rage and plain meanness. But there was something in Cole Anthem's icy stare that forced Jay Lee's brother to rein in his temper.

"Go fetch the horses," Cole said.

Zack grudgingly did as he was told. Behind him, Jay Lee groaned. Two fingers on his left hand had been shot away. His left ear was a tattered flap of meat. He searched the surrounding woods, his face wide-eyed and filled with dread.

"Is it safe?" Jay Lee asked in a plaintive voice thick with suffering.

"Hell no," said Cole.

9

★

"Here. Take a swig of this," McKane said, kneeling by Jay Lee and passing him a jug of brew. The wounded man drank deep while the sergeant finished bandaging his hand. His bloody left ear had already begun to coagulate. "Red Shields left your thumb. Be a plumb nuisance to have a thumb shot off."

Cole entered the circle of warmth emanating from the campfire. He had secured the horses. Now he was curious to discover just what had happened. "How'd you boys wind up like this?" he asked.

"Tain't none of your business," Zack spoke in a surly voice. He buckled on his gunbelt and stood next to his brother.

Jay Lee lowered the jug and passed it to Zack. "Man's got a right," the older brother said. He winced as a spasm of pain coursed the length of his left arm. "After all, Mr. Anthem and his friends did save our lives. The savages snuck up on the post, killed Pa and Becca. We got away, but then got took prisoners by Raven and Young Bull." His voice drifted off as he noticed Dollard rummaging among the Indian's belongings. The scout found a fringed leather parfleche that was suspiciously heavy.

"Damn!" Zack had also spied the scout and charged the man holding the parfleche. He snatched the pouch from Dollard's grasp.

"That's ours!"

The flap ripped open and a shower of gold dust spilled onto the snow. Zack fell to his knees and began shoveling the dust—snow, mud and all—back into the parfleche. "Them braves took it off'n pa. It's ours, by rights."

The sharp, ominous click of Dollard's Colt froze Zack in mid-effort. Still on his knees, he looked up into the barrel of Dollard's gun.

"I don't hold with being laid hand on," Dollard said. "Now I'll take that pouch."

"It's Pa's gold. There ain't much of it. Just enough for me and Jay Lee to start over somewheres else." Zack's eyes darted about the clearing, making a silent appeal for reason and justice.

"He's right," Jay Lee said. "You can see Pa's markings on the pouch. G. H. See for yourselves."

Ben Wheatley, who had been warming himself by the fire, backed out of harm's way. "He's right, I see the initials."

"Stay out of this, nigger," the scout snarled.

Wheatley's expression hardened, but he said nothing. Confrontation would only prove that two men could be twice as foolish as one.

"Holster your gun, Dollard," Cole said. He didn't

care much for the Hammonds but he liked Dollard even less. "Appears the gold is theirs. If you want it otherwise, wait till we reach Fort Conrad."

Dollard held his stance for a moment more, but a look over his shoulder at the guns Cole and McKane had trained on him convinced him to wait and bide his time. He relaxed, walked back to the fire, and put away his gun.

"Sorry. Maybe I went a little crazy, you know what I mean," he said in an ameliorative tone.

Zack grinned and winked at Jay Lee. He slung the parfleche from his belt, gave it a pat, and headed for the fire. Things were finally looking up. He knelt by the coals and looked at Wheatley.

"Better put some grub on, boy. My stomach's a'gnawing on my backbone."

"No time for that," Cole said, closing in. He shoveled snow onto the fire with the toe of his boot.

"Hey!" Zack angrily retorted.

"No telling who heard those shots. We've hung around here long enough," Cole explained.

"But we're cold and hungry," Zack protested.

"And hurting," Jay Lee added.

"Hurting's better than being dead," the bounty hunter replied, and he started for the horses. "We'll have to take turns riding double."

Zack watched the Texan saunter off. Ben Wheatley followed. Then Sam Dollard, with a shrug, joined in. Zack stood, looking forlornly at the buried campfire. He caught McKane by the arms as the sergeant walked by, cradling his Springfield, a plug of tobacco bulging his cheek.

"Who put the likes of Anthem in charge?"

"Oh . . . that buck yonder, for one," McKane said, nodding toward Raven's corpse at the base of a tree a few yards away. The trooper spat in the snow, grinned, and continued on his way.

The six men managed to round a steep, heavily wooded mountainside, and put a glacier-carved ridge between themselves and the two dead Cheyenne braves. The temperature fell with the sun, and snow that had begun to melt refroze while the night was young.

A campfire lapped merrily at the base of a rocky outcropping. The granite backdrop not only partly obscured the blaze but reflected its warmth. The Indian ponies, now ground hobbled, pawed through the snow to uncover the spring shoots of grass rooted in the high country soil.

The trees were sparse here and, save for a few ghostly tendrils of clouds floating on the night, a star-studded panoply stretched from one range of mountains to the other and the length of the broad, winding valley in the heart of which the men had made camp.

Cole Anthem had climbed a hillside and was keeping watch on the back trail when he heard someone crunching through the snow. He turned and recognized Ben Wheatley trailing the set of tracks the Texan had left in the snow.

Wheatley paused to reconsider whether or not he

ought to disturb Cole's silent vigil. But there was something he needed to say, so he continued on until he reached the place where Cole had perched himself on the lightning-blasted remains of a toppled pine.

"You mind me intruding?" Ben asked.

"It's a free country," Cole replied. He sat on the log, his carbine across his lap, his elbows propped on his knees as he studied the moonlit terrain lying to the south.

"I'm sorry about today," the black man said, his eyes downcast. "You cautioned me to hold fire. But when I came face-to-face with that Cheyenne . . . well, I panicked."

"Don't blame you," Cole chuckled. "The bastard scared the hell out of me, too." He glanced up at Wheatley. "Being scared comes pretty natural. But it's what you do with your fear that counts. The way I see it, you could have turned mother's picture to the wall and lit out, instead you kept a'coming. That makes you a man to stand with."

"Thanks," Ben said. The matter was settled and he felt relieved. "I'll keep watch if you want to get on down to the fire and claim your share of the beans and side meat. That is, if Jay Lee left you any."

"His wounds haven't hurt his appetite none, huh?"

" 'Tis not the meat, 'tis the appetite makes eating a delight,' " Ben quoted. "From the works of Sir John Suckling."

"If Jay Lee ate my supper, I'll carve a roast out of his fat rump." The Texan stood and started down the hill. "From the works of Cole Tyler Anthem."

* * *

The faces of the men in firelight looked strained. Their eyes were red-rimmed and pouchy. Their expressions betrayed the toll of constant vigilance and unbroken tension. Cole finished what food had been left him in the skillet and helped himself to a cup of strong black coffee.

"Where we bound now?" Sergeant McKane said at last. "Reckon we ought to try and hook up with Major Busby's detachment."

"And run into Medicine Bear and his main force? Not hardly." Cole sloshed some of the coffee grounds from his cup.

"Morgan's Landing," McKane said, reading Anthem's thoughts. It was the only other choice. "If we start early and keep our horses lathered, we can make the Rogue River sometime late tomorrow."

"I think we should turn tail and make a run south, plumb out of this territory," Dollard said.

"I'm with Dollard," Zack interjected. "Me and Jay Lee both."

"How far do you think you'd get riding double?" Cole asked.

Zack pondered a moment. It dawned on him that four horses were more than enough for Dollard and the Hammonds.

"I just saw something in your eyes," Anthem said in a quiet, ominous voice. "I just saw a real fool thought flash across your face."

Zack shrugged, coughed nervously, taken aback by

Cole's murderous tone. "Look. What good's that old horse-faced bitch, Morgan, to us?"

"She's got a keelboat," McKane explained. "The Rogue runs into the Marias and straight to Fort Conrad and more U.S. soldiers than even Medicine Bear could take. Looks like we'll end this thing up sailors, yessir." The sergeant slapped his thigh and laughed aloud.

"What makes you think Morgan will still be there?" Jay Lee spoke up from his blankets. He took care to prop himself up with his good right hand. "She might have already been killed by Cheyennes."

"It's worth the gamble," Cole said.

"I'm for it," added Ben Wheatley, approaching out of the surrounding darkness. The strength of his assertion surprised even him. He took his place by the fire. "I believe it's time I was spelled." He looked around at the Hammond brothers who stared at him as if the black man had committed the utmost effrontery by daring to offer an opinion.

Zack met Anthem's solemn gaze and snorted in disgust. He spat in the fire, his phlegm sizzling. "Seein' as we ain't got no choice, my brother and me will tag along," he acquiesced, his mood souring.

Jay Lee seemed to want to dispute the fact further, but his brother immediately stretched out on his blanket and closed his eyes. Jay Lee wanted to get as far from the authorities as possible. The murder of his father weighed heavily on his nerves. He wouldn't feel safe until he was completely out of the territory.

"I'll stand the next watch," Sam Dollard volunteered. He took up his Henry rifle and sauntered toward the hillside.

Anthem watched the scout depart as did McKane.

"Maybe we oughta hobble Sam as well as those ponies," the sergeant muttered.

"My thoughts exactly," Cole replied. He settled back on a crudely woven mat of pine boughs. He planned to rest for just a minute or two.

"I'll keep an eye out," McKane said, again sensing Cole's concern. "Get some rest, you've slept less than any of us."

"Irish, you have an uncanny knack for reading a man's mind," said Anthem, yawning.

"That's why I'm a sergeant," McKane confessed. "It's a talent that comes with the stripes."

Cole nodded in appreciation. He was dead tired. He closed his eyes and sleep came easy.

10

The campfire crackled and in the distance a wolf howled. Near the circle of firelight a pair of snow-shoe hares paused to scent the sleeping men, then darted off among the trees. Overhead, the rush of wings in the black sky pursued them.

Cole Anthem was oblivious to the night. He dreamt of chestnut hair and eyes the color of the sky after a spring rain, pale blue with a hint of turquoise. Small breasts, easy to cup and kiss. Glory arched against him and he entered her.

"More," she whispered, "more." And when she shuddered, "Oh my sweet, my sweet," her strong thighs captured him and held his hard strength as the fire in him poured forth.

She was Glory Doolin of Missouri. He was Cole Tyler Anthem of Texas. They were bounty hunters. And they were lovers.

It was good to lie back in the warmth while the hard edges of life were smoothed and wounds were healed. They were good for each other's souls.

Cole rolled on his back and sighed. Glory scrunched down in the covers and nuzzled his neck and bit playfully at his ear. They lay naked and entwined on rumpled white sheets, and when at last the chill of night stole upon their haven and the last log in the fireplace crackled and split, Glory pulled a thick down comforter up to their chins.

Outside beyond the walls of Hanna's Inn, a lone coyote darted across the wheel rutted road that led to Denver, three miles away. The animal scampered up through the aspens until it reached a ledge of table rock. It settled there on its haunches and bayed at the night sky. A song of loneliness, of loss, a melancholy for a changing world.

"Don't go in to Denver. Stay here with me," said Cole.

"And do what?" Glory rolled on to his chest, her nipples like hard little berries against his skin.

"Guess," said Cole.

"And when we both ran out of money Dee Hanna would throw us out. We aren't rich cattlemen and stock raisers like the rest of her boarders." Glory draped her shoulder-length hair across his chest and playfully whipped him with her silken tresses. He caught her by the throat and pulled her down to his lips.

Glory pulled back. "You could come with me. Sam Dollard's worth seven hundred dollars. We could split it equal shares, four hundred apiece."

"That comes to eight hundred," Cole corrected.

"Well then three hundred for you," Glory laughed and tweaked his nose.

"I've tired of it, Glory. Anyway, you don't need me to catch the likes of this Dollard."

"No," Glory conceded. "He has a weakness for soiled doves and that's just what I'll be until I clap him in irons and take him back to Kansas City to hang." She pursed her lips, her eyebrows arched playfully. She seemed so innocent and girlish.

"You won't quit. You'll see," she said. "We're alike, Cole. And this is what we do best. We can't change . . . won't change till they put us under." Glory's hands slid down his chest and stomach. "And I intend to live till I die, Cole Tyler Anthem," she said.

This man Dollard wouldn't know what hit him, Cole figured. So he held her close and listened to the cry of the coyote. Before Glory drifted off to sleep she laughed softly, kissed his shoulder, smiled wantonly, and said, "Don't worry, Cole. I never met a man I couldn't take."

But she had never met Sam Dollard.

Cole, still dreaming, watched as Glory was transformed, her cheeks became shrunken, her flesh pale and bloodless. The smile was gone, becoming thin-lipped, weak, the look of a woman at the brink of death . . . because of Sam Dollard—

Cole snapped awake. His hand dropped to the carbine at his side. The stars above continued to glimmer. He checked the campfire, noticed the blaze needed tending, and gauged he'd been asleep for an hour.

Maybe two. Anthem sat upright, heard a guttural snore and saw it came from Danny McKane. The sergeant had propped himself against the granite ledge. His chin dug into his chest, his head rising and falling with each breath.

"Damn," the bounty hunter cursed beneath his breath and rolled off his bedding. He stood beyond the glare of the campfire, waiting, listening and allowing his vision to adjust to the darkness. Out on the meadow and near a grove of spruces that served as a windbreak, the horses stirred and whinnied nervously as someone or something approached them. Back by the fire, Zack Hammond grumbled in his sleep and rolled over on his side. Anthem studied the sleeping man and realized that Hammond's gold pouch no longer hung from the young man's belt. Cole hefted his Winchester and trotted across the snow.

The footing was treacherous. The temperature had dropped well below freezing and the snow bore a layer of ice an inch thick. Cole ran a few yards, listened, ran again, and then paused as some fifteen yards to the right, a man plodded out from between two Douglas firs and brought up sharply. It could only be Dollard. Cole wondered if he was as visible against the stark white snowscape as the scout. His question was answered almost immediately as Dollard broke into a dread run toward the horses.

Cole moved to cut him off, lost his footing, and skidded to one knee. He stood again and broke into a dread run, chancing a nasty fall on the hardened snow. Dollard was quick but Cole's long legged gait closed the gap. The scout reached the horses first. They neighed and turned skittish and tried to plunge away from him but their hobbled forelegs kept them from getting far. Still, the frightened animals pawed the air and flailed at the earth as Dollard tried first one half wild mount, then another. On his third try he caught a handful of horse hair rope around the neck of a sorrel. Setting aside his Henry rifle, Dollard drew his knife and severed the rawhide hobbles, freeing the animal's legs. The horses tried to pull up and make a mad dash for safety but the scout kept a tight grip on the rope. Forsaking his rifle, he swung up onto the sorrel's bare back and drove his booted heels into the animal's flanks.

Cole, running flat out, dove through the air and hurled himself like a cannon shot against the sorrel's neck. Reaching up, Anthem caught a handful of mane and twisted the animal's head down and under the momentum of his leap. The sorrel lost its footing in the slick surface of the meadow and went down.

Sam Dollard kicked free and went sprawling on his belly like a skipped stone. Cole rolled out of the way of the horse's deadly hooves as the sorrel fell on its side and raked the air. Cole held onto the Indian pony's ears and mane and tried to calm the frightened creature. Words failed but Cole bought himself time enough to tie his bandana across the sorrel's eyes. Anthem shoved free, scrambled up, and came face to face with Sam Dollard.

Dollard was smaller than Cole by half a foot and forty pounds, but he was quick and strong, a brawler whose left fist almost whistled as it sliced through space. Cole twisted about to allow his shoulder to take the brunt of the blow. Then he closed in and drove his knee between the scout's legs. Dollard doubled with pain and sank to his knees, his breath rasping in his throat.

"I was hoping you'd start something," Cole said, the dream of Glory Doolin still fresh in his mind.

The scout shook his head and groaned as he looked up at Anthem. "You've done some back street fightin'," said Dollard. "Oh . . . shit . . . just who the hell are you?" His hand flirted with the worn wooden grip of his Colt.

"Touch that gun and you'll find out, Cole said. He'd dropped the Winchester in order to catch the sorrel and doubted he could out draw the likes of Sam Dollard. The bounty hunter's only recourse was to bluff the scout. It worked.

Dollard changed his mind. He was curious but not enough to chance dying just to satisfy that curiosity. He bent double, dug his hands into the snow for support, braced himself, and tried to catch his breath.

Cole Anthem, confident now, knelt opposite the man.

"Tell me, Dollard. Just how much did Medicine Bear offer to pay you?"

"What the hell . . . you . . . mean by that?"

'You know, for leading the survey party into a trap. Although when it came time to collect you found out what his word is worth to a white man."

"You bastard," Dollard wheezed. "Soon as . . . I get

my balls . . . out of my backside I'll make . . . you eat them words." His features, already contorted from pain, grew livid.

Cole shrugged. "I could be wrong. You might have simply turned yellow and lit out when the Red Shields arrived. Of course, desertion is a hanging offense, even for a scout."

"Goddamn you," Dollard roared. His winded state had been a ruse. Suddenly his hands flew upward, shoveling a mixture of ice, snow, and dirt into Anthem's face.

Blinded, the bounty hunter tried to stand. Dollard lunged forward and head-butted Cole beneath the rib cage. The Texan crashed over on his backside.

Dollard landed on top of him. Cole squirmed and managed to work his right arm out from under the weight of the scout. Through his damaged vision Cole caught the glimmer of a knife blade. His hand snaked out and caught the wrist of Dollard's knife hand. Undaunted, the scout applied his free hand and put all his leverage behind the knife. "I'll show you," the scout growled through clenched teeth. "You'll wear my brand for the rest of your days."

Cole concentrated on his arm, willing the muscles into iron and yet despite his strength, he yielded. Ever so slowly the point of the knife lowered toward his forehead. Anthem closed his eyes and focused all his concentration on resisting the gleaming blade's inexorable descent. He tried to work loose his left arm but Dollard's knees had him pinned tight.

The scout had ceased to speak. He needed every

ounce of energy to overcome the Texan. Dollard was surprised at Cole's strength. But Sam knew he had the upper hand and it was only a matter of time, just a few more seconds and he'd overpower this trouble-maker and be done with it. And there'd be nothing between Sam Dollard and New Mexico but distance. He had the gold, he had horses, he had everything a man needed for the trail.

The muzzle of a Springfield rifle planted its cold steel kiss against the side of Dollard's neck. The scout stiffened at the touch and the triumph welling in his breast faded as he turned to look along the barrel and up into the ebony face of Ben Wheatley.

" 'To be or not to be,' " said Ben. "That, Mr. Dollard, is your question." The black man glanced down at the breechloader in his hands. "Now, I've only fired this rifle once but I think I got the hang of it. Let's see, I squeeze this trigger here, and a bullet comes out there, and splatters your brains all over the snow."

Caught off guard by Wheatley's arrival on the scene, the scout eased his hold, and Anthem took advantage of the situation to heave upward and shove Dollard clear. Cole was as surprised as the scout to see Ben Wheatley, gun in hand, play the role of rescuer. But he was a welcome sight.

"I woke up as you were leaving camp," Ben explained. "And I took a notion to follow."

"Black bastard," Dollard growled as he clambered to his feet. "So now what?"

Cole stepped in, took the scout's knife and cut free

the pouch of gold dust. Then he tucked the blade back into Dollard's beaded buckskin sheath.

"We still need you, Sam," said Anthem. And he smiled a smile without warmth. "All the way to Fort Conrad."

"Yeah, and what happens then?"

"You find out who the hell I am."

The camp was still quiet. McKane and the Hammonds were sleeping soundly. Dollard crawled into his bedroll, turned his back to the fire, and lay quiet. He had a score to settle with Ben Wheatley. The black would pay for his interference. Like Anthem would pay. They both owed Sam Dollard now, and the scout always collected his debts. He closed his eyes and began to plan the ways.

Cole Anthem nudged the snoring figure of Zack Hammond, who surfaced from a deep sleep all asputter and uncertain of his surroundings. Disorientation faded at the sight of the buckskin parfleche dangling from Cole's grasp.

Hammond bolted upright. Cole dropped the gold on the ground next to the newly awakened young man.

"You better sleep a little lighter," Cole cautioned.

"Wha . . . ?" Zack demanded, snatching up the pouch and cradling it in his protective embrace. Wild-eyed, he suspected everyone of betrayal. "What the hell happened?"

Cole glanced in Dollard's direction, shrugged, and held up his empty hands, palms out. "A snake tried to steal it."

11

The Rogue River was fed by myriad springs and creeks and the melted snow of glacial ridges and jagged peaks. It flowed eastward and eventually turned south to join the Marias River on its winding journey eastward to merge at last with the Missouri.

Back on the wooden fringe masking a glacier-sculpted ridge on the river's south bank, six men waited and watched. They scrutinized the scene below as if their lives depended on it, which was the case.

Cole Anthem studied Morgan's Landing for signs of life and was rewarded at last as a small, fiesty woman appeared around the corner of the blockhouse that served as her home and headquarters.

Captain Andy Morgan shook her fist at a war party of eight Cheyenne who had retreated across the meadow to the protection of the trees. She hoisted what appeared to be a burlap sack over her shoulder and sauntered toward her keelboat docked at the river's edge at the end of a rather treacherous-looking plank walkway.

Andy Morgan's boat was a sharp-nosed craft fully sixty feet in length and twelve feet wide with walkways to either side and a flat-roofed common cabin dominating the center of the craft. The word "Valhalla" (Andy was partial to Norse mythology) had been painted on the bow.

A hard, flint-faced woman, Morgan was diminutive but tough enough to captain a crew and bring her boat up the Rogue to set up trade with both the trappers and the Indians. The Cheyennes and Blackfeet had allowed her to remain once the tribes had acquired a taste for blankets, beads and bolts of bright cloth. Cole figured the situation was pretty serious if the likes of Morgan's Landing, which red men and white considered neutral ground, was now under siege.

"What do you think, lad?" Sergeant McKane asked, keeping his voice low. The Indians below were about a hundred yards from the landing and about twice that from the men on the ridge. Of course, none of the braves were riding double.

Cole continued to watch in silence as Andy emerged from the cabin and leaped onto the rickety pier jutting from the steep bank into the river.

Great flat irregular chunks of ice floated by. The river had begun to break up despite the late spring storm. The Rogue still was frigid, an azure waterway some twenty yards across. Here it had cut a gorge in the riverbend. The south bank where Andy had set up, offered the sharpest bluff. The north bank was more eroded and prone to landslide and flood. Few trees grew here to root the soil in place.

"How do you want to play it?" McKane asked, deferring to Anthem's judgment. To the sergeant's way of thinking, Cole was the man to follow in a fight.

"I say we wait till under cover of night and sneak on down to the landing," Zack suggested.

"We might risk losing Andy's boat. She looks as if she's getting ready to cut and run," said Cole.

"I didn't fancy bein' no goddamn sailor anyhow." Zack shrugged.

"You're a fool, Hammond," said Cole. "That boat is our only chance out of this mess. You really think Medicine Bear is riding his war trail alone? These mountains are primed for war. I've seen the sign. Indian villages are on the move. Something big is happening. Medicine Bear is massing all the Red Shield clans under his banner." Ben and the sergeant stared at him.

"C'mon," he said, and started descending the wooded slope.

"You mean, we just ride on down to the Landing like those red painted devils weren't even there," Dollard exclaimed. He shook his head. "Madness!"

"The odds are pretty square," Cole said. "Only one of them has a rifle. Those elkhorn bows they're carrying don't have the range to hit us before we hit them. They'd be crazy to try to stop us." Anthem glanced at the keelboat. If they waited until dark and Morgan pulled out without them, it would be a disaster.

"Sure and I'm bone tired of running past these bastards," Sergeant McKane said. "I'd fancy strutting on past and thumbin' me nose at the blood-thirsty heathens." The Irishman scratched the five day silver stubble that made his cheeks and jaw as rough as sandpaper. He cocked his Springfield and glanced over his shoulder at the black man riding directly behind him. Zack and Jay Lee also rode double, leaving Dollard, like Cole, to ride alone.

"I hate to admit it," the scout said, "but Anthem's right." He looked over at the Hammonds. "Come along, boys. That gold won't buy you spit in hell with your heads decorating a couple of Red Shield lances."

"You just keep your distance from us and this here parfleche," Zack warned, patting the gun holstered on his thigh in warning.

"Down yonder is your enemy." Dollard feigned innocence. "The way I see it, you boys might be needing me for a friend."

"What the hell do you mean by that," Jay Lee muttered.

"Only that I know how Gus Hammond came by his gold. And I have a good idea how you boys ended up with it, too." He levered a shell into the chamber of his Henry. Tube fed, the rifle held fifteen rounds. It was said a man with such a rifle could load on Monday and shoot all week.

Zack and Jay Lee exchanged worried glances. And Dollard chuckled, knowing he had struck a nerve with the men. He might finish up his Army career with a profit after all.

"Don't worry boys. I'm a man who respects ambition," Sam's gaze turned lean and hungry. "After all, I'm an ambitious man myself."

*   *   *

"Hey, Ben . . . I forgot to thank you for saving my life
the other night," Cole said as he walked his pony out
into the meadow. Ben Wheatley, sitting uncomfortably
behind the sergeant, waved at the bounty hunter. The
black man's attention was focused on the war party at
the edge of the trees. The Cheyenne had spotted the
new arrivals and fanned out as if to swoop down on
them.

"Feel free to pull my fat out of the fire whenever
you feel like it," Cole continued, distracting Wheatley
and easing the ex-slave's apprehension. Cole felt as
naked as any of them. They were inviting trouble and
he knew it. The horses were too tired to run. Though
these Red Shields were not as well armed and the odds
did not favor them, honor was a strong motivation and
often led men to take chances.

The war party started forward, trotting their horses,
into the meadow. A bell began to peel, clanging merrily from the roof of the blockhouse. Andy Morgan
was welcoming them. But the Cheyenne were moving
to intersect the intruders. The horses carrying double
would never make it. The Red Shield mounts were
fresh and fleet of foot. The red-painted braves cried
out, taunting and challenging what they took to be a
helpless, bedraggled band of survivors.

"Tell me, Ben," Cole said, angling over to the horse
ridden by McKane and Wheatley. "You must know a
quote for a situation like this."

Wheatley thought a moment and searched his memory for a suitable phrase. He settled on *Henry the Fifth*.

" 'But when the blast of war blows in our ears, / Then imitate the action of a tiger; / Stiffen the sinews, summon up the blood, / Disguise fair nature with hard-favored rage!' " He looked from the oncoming braves back to Cole. "How's that?" he asked.

"I couldn't have said it better myself." Cole grinned. Suddenly he drove his heels into the flanks of his horse. The animal bolted past the other three. "Head for the landing," he shouted at his companions.

The carbine's brass frame glittered in the sunlight as Cole charged through the snow-covered buffalo grass and headed straight for the startled braves. The Hammonds, Dollard, and McKane urged their horses to a gallop and pointed them straight for the blockhouse.

Ben leaned out and leaped from his horse to the back of Sam Dollard's mount before the scout could pull away. Ben snatched the Henry repeater from the startled man's grasp.

"What the hell are you doing?" Dollard shouted over his shoulder. He struggled to retrieve his rifle and lost his balance.

"Practicing what I preach," Wheatley said and shoved the scout from horseback. He wheeled the animal about and raced after Cole as Dollard landed face-first in the snow. He clambered to his feet, sputtering rage.

"You black bastard!" Dollard shouted. He grabbed for his gun then realized he was afoot and easy prey

for the war party if they got past Cole. The scout
cussed and broke into a desperate run for Morgan's
Landing.

Anthem rapidly closed the gap with the war party.
He pulled up just out of range of the Red Shield's
elkhorn bows. Settling the Winchester's stock against
his shoulder, he snapped off a couple of rounds,
shifted his aim, and loosed another three shots. A warrior doubled over and, clinging to the neck of his
horse, rode out of the fray.

Cole continued firing and was surprised by the
deeper roar of Ben Wheatley's rifle off to his left. A
second brave pitched from his horse and skidded
across the ground, leaving a trail of scarlet snow in
his wake. Riding hard, a third brave charged headlong
through the scattering Cheyenne. The warrior lowered
his lethal-looking spear and loosed a wild cry that a
slug from the Henry cut short. The brave straightened
as the bullet struck him square in the quill breastplate.

The Winchester Yellowboy followed the Henry. It
spoke again and finished the warrior, who tumbled
from horseback and buried his spear in the earth as he
landed belly down on the hard-packed meadow and
rolled half a dozen feet before flip-flopping face up,
his dead eyes staring.

Of the five remaining braves now melting into the
forest shadows on the opposite edge of the meadow,
one walked his painted stallion from the field of battle.
He was High-Backed Wolf, too proud to run, too wise
to risk certain death charging his hated enemy with
their repeating rifles.

High-Backed Wolf carried the Sharps buffalo rifle he had taken from the Hammond ranch. He had fired it only once and the empty cartridge was jammed in the breach. He would have to extract it with his knife. The brave paused and faced the two men who had driven off the attacking Cheyenne. He raised the Sharps over his head, held it aloft, and cried out to them in his native tongue. He taunted them and challenged the *ve-ho-e* to pursue him. He spat on the ground and walked his horse in tight circles to demonstrate his horsemanship and skill as a warrior. The Cheyenne told the white men their scalps would soon be hanging from his belt. Then, mustering every ounce of dignity he possessed, he solemnly turned and disappeared into the woods.

Across the meadow, Cole watched him leave. Then he glanced over at the man at his side. "You are a wealth of surprises, Mr. Wheatley."

Ben shook his head, wiped the perspiration from his brow, and sighed in relief. "Even to myself, Mr. Anthem," he chuckled.

Cole nodded and returned his attention to the forest's edge.

"I guess we showed them," Ben bravely added.

"We haven't shown them anything they haven't seen before," Cole said. He looked up at the cloudless sky. The sun beat down upon the snow-carpeted landscape. Rivulets of icy water ran beneath the gradually diminishing snowy surface.

"You think they'll be back?" Wheatley asked, a note of apprehension creeping back into his voice.

"Maybe tonight, or they might lick their wounds till sunup," Cole said.

"But I thought Indians didn't fight at night," Ben snapped. His knowledge of Indians was derived from dime novels he had found on newsstands in Boston.

"An Indian will fight anytime," Cole drily observed. "With anyone. And anywhere, within reason." He jabbed a thumb toward the forest. "Cheyenne Red Shields haven't read about themselves in the penny dreadfuls so they don't know how they're supposed to fight proper."

Cole shaded his eyes, stared at the sun, estimated the time of day, and wondered if Andy could have them aboard the *Valhalla* and floating down the Rogue before dusk. With any luck at all . . .

The world began to spin. Cole shut his eyes and willed the world to stop, to lock into place. When he opened his eyes, the world had obeyed. He wiped the perspiration from his forehead and felt the scabbed head wound that was the legacy of his faked suicide. Maybe he better ease up and take his time here at the landing.

"You all right, Cole?" Ben asked, walking his horse alongside the bounty hunter.

Cole appraised the man next to him. *I wonder if I look as bone tired and haggard as Ben.*

"Cole?"

"Yeah. I'm fine. Nothing that a full belly and a warm woman couldn't cure." Cole looked toward the blockhouse. McKane and the others had reached Morgan's Landing and were arranged in front of the long, low-roofed log building that served as Andy Morgan's storehouse and fortress. Anthem had only visited it once before during his stay in the mountain country. The survey party had bivouacked there a couple of weeks ago. Its furnishings were spare at best and Andy could be cantankerous. But after so many days of dodging Cheyenne war parties, Morgan's Landing seemed like a haven of safety.

Where was the harm in a few extra hours of rest? Cole reconsidered. They all needed it. And the days that lay ahead did not exactly promise to be a Sunday outing.

Sudden silence engulfed them. A pair of bald eagles circled in the azure sky. Below, the snow-blanketed meadow glistened as if it were strewn with diamonds. Only the two dead men, their blood staining the snow, spoiled the virginal scene. Ben glanced at the rifle in his hands, the realization dawning that he had taken a life.

In silence Cole turned and started toward the landing. And Ben, leaving the dead men behind with his guilt, followed after.

Andy Morgan was a woman of fifty, leather skinned, hawk nosed and tough as nails. She and her keelboat had become a legend along the Rogue. Sprightly as a twenty-year-old, she ran up to greet Cole, and offered him a drink from a half-gallon jug of homebrew.

"I knew there was a reason I took a shine to you the first time you came through, Cole Anthem," Andy exclaimed. She tucked a graying strand of hair up in-

side her floppy-brimmed hat and flashed him a broad
smile that revealed a row of strong white teeth marred
by a chipped incisor. Her brown eyes gazed at him, a
hint of wistfulness in her expression. McKane, the
Hammonds, and Sam Dollard had already filed inside
the building, eager to fill their bellies with her stew
and chase away the jitters with a whiskey or two. A
slim, bespectacled gentleman in tattered finery approached as Cole and Wheatley dismounted. He extended a pale hand toward Cole.

"This is Silas Dean," Andy explained. "He's from
the East, so he tells me. Claims to be a writer. He
showed up on Matt Trainer's wagon. Trainer got hisself killed along with his girls; all but one that is. She
came in with Silas."

Cole was trying to assimilate all of what Andy was
telling him. Here were clearly more fugitives from
Medicine Bear's war parties. What of Busby's command at work on the new outpost? Matt Trainer ran
whores to the soldiers, followed troops wherever they
went. He had followed Busby and been killed. His
death was no great loss, but the implications were dangerous. Before Cole could press Andy for more infor-
mation, Silas Dean shook his hand.

"That was a most dramatic confrontation, Mr. Anthem. May I call you Cole? I should like to interview
you later on. You and your friend." Dean nodded toward the black man. Ben started to offer a reply, but
the words caught in his throat at the sight of the
woman who came to stand next to Dean. She was a
mulatto, and beautiful despite the oversized woolen

shirt and trousers covering her lithe frame.

"Ah, and this is my friend and companion in misery. We escaped, as you can see, with little more than the clothes on our backs," said Silas, tucking the threadbare cuff of his shirt into his ragged coat sleeve.

"Some of us with even less than that," the mulatto said as she brushed her long black hair out of her eyes, cocked a hip, and after a monetary appraisal of Ben Wheatley, looked up at Cole, a hint of recognition in her eyes. "Folks call me Journey," she added.

"Funny name for a girl," Ben Wheatley commented, stepping up beside Cole.

"Not if you've been there," she replied.

"Where?"

"On a journey," the mulatto winked at the younger man then fixed her provocative stare at Anthem. "Hello Cole."

"Have—have you two met?" Silas stammered, annoyed at the idea of competition.

"A few years back," Journey said. "In Arkansas, a town called Teardrop." She moistened her lips. "Cole was scarcely more than a boy . . . well . . . a boy and a man all at once."

"The war had a way of doing that," Cole said. "I remember you." He could read the jealousy in the writer's eyes and added, "We were scarce more than acquaintances."

Silas grudgingly relaxed. "How nice."

Ben, however, took Journey's hand, bowed and kissed it. "Ma'am, your presence makes the past ordeal almost worthwhile. I hope you'll favor me with

a few moments of pleasant conversation over dinner."
He bowed again, and, oblivious to Silas Dean's angry
glare, gestured toward the blockhouse.

"My, such gallantry," Journey laughed. "Manners
are an uncommon pleasure." She hooked her arm in
Ben's and walked with him up the steps and into the
blockhouse.

Cole wagged his head in astonishment at the almost
courtly way young Ben Wheatley had taken Journey
in tow. "Ben may be a pilgrim out here in the mountains, but I'll warrant he's a regular curly wolf in the
drawing room." He noted a scowl had returned to Silas
Dean's features."

"Trouble is," Andy replied, "I think he's charting
territory that's already claimed." She nudged Cole and
winked. "C'mon, Mr. Dean. I'll buy you a drink. And
you can make me feel younger than I am."

"What . . . oh . . . yes. A drink. One or two might
be in order," Silas glumly replied. His displeasure
abated somewhat as he returned his attention to Cole.
"Now tell me Mr. Anthem . . . just how long have you
been an Indian fighter?"

Cole glanced back toward the meadow, its snowy
surface criss-crossed with tracks. "About thirty
minutes, I'd say."

Dean looked crestfallen, his dreams of being the
next Ned Buntline fading.

"Uh . . . surely a man of your capabilities . . . I
mean, well," Silas retorted, refusing to abandon his
dream. "Tell me, what do you hold as your most sin-
gular achievement here in the howling wilderness?"

Cole started down the path toward the blockhouse, and his answer trailed back to the writer. A simple two-word reply.

"Staying alive."

12

Corporal Philippe DuToit had once been a captain of infantry in the Franco-Prussian War. The fall of Paris had dashed his dream of a military career in his native country. Fleeing Prussian domination, DuToit had landed in New Orleans. From there he had wandered north with the river. Depressed, and missing the military life, he had enlisted in the Dakotas. Corporal wasn't much of a rank, and there were times Philippe grieved on account of his personal plummet from the vaulted heights of military aristocracy. At such times he tended to drink too much. Now was such a time. It softened his fall from prominence, soothed his damaged ego. And one thing more: He drank to forget how frightened he was. For Philippe DuToit had lost more than his rank, he had lost his nerves as well. Fear gnawed at his vitals, leaving him a wrecked shell of a man, a hollow man desperately trying to overcome his cowardice.

DuToit was a man of average height, but broad-shouldered and with coarse thick features. A thick black mustache covered his lower lip and flowed up to curl across his cheeks. He was forever twisting the tips of his mustache, an action he assumed whenever he was telling a story. He enjoyed being the center of attention and he milked such moments for all they were worth. Now he leaned back against the bar, a stoneware cup of home-brewed whiskey in his hand. He sloshed the contents onto the floor with each broad gesture. His booming voice filled the room.

"Busby never knew what happened," DuToit said. "I saw him myself drop to the ground with one, two, three arrows in his heart." He mimicked the sound of the arrows striking home and his eyes rolled back in his head as he gasped.

He paused to allow for effect and took the opportunity to gauge his audience. The Hammonds were seated at one table, watching the Frenchman with disinterest. Sam Dollard stood at the bar, wolfing down a plate of stew. He gave no indication of listening to DuToit's account.

Cole was standing near a shuttered window, a slab of meat and bread in one hand, strong black coffee in the other as he peered through a peephole, keeping a constant check on the meadow. He didn't trust the Red Shields to remain at a distance, even though he felt certain the braves wouldn't try anything until night.

DuToit turned to the only audience who seemed to be paying him any mind: Ben Wheatley, Journey, Sergeant McKane. The two men were already on their second bowls of stew while Journey was nursing a drink, taking little sips and casting hooded glances in

Wheatley's direction. Behind them at another table, Silas Dean drank and fumed.

"The savages were among the tents in an instant. *Sacre*, such slaughter!" DuToit gave a dramatic shudder. "The Prussian may be a wretched animal but at least he is a Christian. These red devils, red like demons from Hell. What manner of foe is this? And how they enjoy their butchery."

"Yet you escaped," Andy Morgan said from in back of the bar. She leaned forward and filled the Frenchman's cup.

"But of course, mademoiselle. I drew my saber and charged through their ranks, cutting my way to freedom, killing a savage with every stroke!" He downed the contents of his cup, doubled over and spewed it on the floor. "Pah! Water. Am I a fish you give me water?"

"I'm preparing you for the journey that lies ahead," Andy chuckled, her weathered features crinkling as she smiled. "You'll have a bellyful of the Rogue before you reach Fort Conrad."

"And how did you make your escape?" Ben asked the woman at his side.

Journey leaned in close to him. "Silas and I were . . . alone . . . out in a supply wagon. We ran for our lives. And that old phony came from somewhere to run with us." Journey squeezed the young man's arm and giggled. Ben decided then and there, that despite the baggy clothing, Journey was the most fetching woman he had ever laid eyes on or encountered in all his twenty years.

"Run . . . me?" Philippe blustered. "I was charging, leading the way, sword in hand. I cannot help it if there were no Indians directly in my path."

"Seems to me you ain't nothing' but a fancy talkin' loud mouthed coward," Zack Hammond said from his table near the fireplace. His eyes were red-rimmed, his movements already sluggish from the effect of Morgan's whiskey.

"Yeah," Jay Lee echoed. "Why don't you tell us the truth. You turned yellow and ran." He was feeling more optimistic now about their chances. And the proximity of his father's gold fueled his bravado.

"As long as you Hammond boys are interested in the truth," Andy Morgan began. She stepped around the bar and advanced on the brothers. "Suppose you tell me what a crate marked "tools" your pa had me bring in before the river froze up is doin' full of Henry rifles. Reckon he had Cheyenne gold in mind?"

"Pa, never. That's a lie, you old witch," Zack blurted as he jumped to his feet, knocking the chair he had been sitting in on its side.

"Knocked it open by accident," the river woman cackled. "Figured out what was going on and had them guns so's ol' Gus couldn't lay his hands on 'em." Morgan tilted her head back and started to belly laugh, lapsing instead into a fit of coughing. She slumped down on the closest ladderbacked chair and caught her breath.

"She's crazed. The old witch don't know what she's saying. Pa grubbed his gold out of the creeks!" Zack advanced menacingly on the woman. She watched him with a wary eye and wished she hadn't left the shotgun behind the bar.

It was a big room, built to serve as both a saloon and mercantile with tables and chairs and a hand-hewn log bar on one side of the room, shelves and racks bearing clothes and canned goods and tools on the other. Supplies were low. And the crew to man her boat had failed to rendezvous with her at the landing. Andy Morgan had a keen interest in the people in the room. They were to be her crew. Every man was needed. Even Zack Hammond.

"Have it your own way, Zack," she said, trying to soothe his quick-tempered nature. "Maybe you didn't know. You or your pa."

Zack hooked his thumbs in his gunbelt and nodded. "Damn right," he muttered. He looked around and saw that Andy Morgan's acquiescence had fooled no one. Now they all knew of the rifles. It wouldn't do for such suspicions to reach Fort Conrad. That was a dilemma he'd have to work out later.

He turned and sauntered back to his table, a cocky bounce to his step. He sat down across from his brother and winked, then helped himself to a drink.

"If we're going to get some rest," Cole said. "We'll have to post a watch." A ladder reached up from the main room to a trapdoor in the ceiling. The flat roof above was fortified with a five-foot-high wall around the entire perimeter. A man could keep an eye on things from up above.

"Anyone for first watch?"

"I'll take it," Ben Wheatley spoke up, dabbing the

last of the drippings on his plate with a morsel of bread. "Good vittles, Captain Andy," he added. He stood and started toward the ladder after a courteous bow to Journey.

"Wait up," Morgan said and rose from her place.

She crossed into the mercantile, bent over and dragged out a crate, hauling it, with Cole's help to the center of the room. She knocked the lid off with the flat of her hand.

"These are the Henrys nobody claims. Ya'll better help yourselves. And careful, they're loaded."

"See here," Jay Lee blurted. The Henry rifles represented a considerable amount of wealth, and he had hoped there might be some way of recovering them.

"I can't see the harm," Cole agreed, trying to hide his amusement. "Since they don't belong to anyone in particular." He passed a repeater to Ben, another to McKane. Cole offered one to Silas Dean.

The writer considered the weapon, hesitated, then shrugged. "I have always believed the pen is mightier than the sword. However, as things stand . . ." He sighed and took the long-barreled Henry.

"DuToit, how about you?" Cole asked.

"I prefer the blade," the Frenchman replied, taking up a saber he had left leaning against the bar. "Cut, parry, slash, now that is the way for a gentleman to fight." Metal rasped on metal as he started to unsheathe the blade.

"Only trouble is the Red Shields are fighters, not gentlemen," Cole replied.

"*Mais oui,*" DuToit said and returned the keen-edged weapon to its scabbard. "You are correct. But of course." He took the repeater. "Ah, fifteen rounds before reloading. If we had had such guns in the streets of my beloved Paris, we could have driven back the Prussian bastards."

As Cole distributed the repeating rifles to the remainder of the group, Andy ventured once more among her store goods and returned with several boxes of cartridges. Everyone loaded up.

Ben tucked a fistful of extra shells into his coat pocket and climbed the ladder to the roof. Journey started to follow, but Silas Dean caught her by the arm and pulled her down beside him. Her smile was for him, but her eyes focused past him on the man disappearing through the trap door in the ceiling.

Closing the crate, Cole hammered the lid in place, sealing in the rest of the rifles.

"Aren't you going to take one for yourself?" Andy asked.

"I'll stick with what I got," Cole replied.

"You and that Yellowboy seem made for each other, right enough," Morgan said.

Behind her at the bar, Sam Dollard straightened suddenly and jerked around to stare at Cole. He watched as the Texan started to lift the crate of rifles.

"I'll help with those," Dollard said uncharacteristically. He shoved away from the bar, crossed to the center of the room, and took up the other end of the crate, grabbing the rope handle and lifting with Cole, who had to set his carbine aside. "Lead the way."

* * *

Snow crunched like winter wheat under their boots. Elsewhere in the black gloom of the pines, ice-glazed branches cracked in the brittle cold. The two men struggled with the crate of Henry rifles, as they headed toward the boat.

"Ought not to be this heavy," Sam Dollard said as his bootheels scraped on a wooden plank and he climbed onto the pier, shifting the weight of the crate to Cole a few feet below.

The Texan hoisted his end of the crate chest high and gained the slick walkway. A minute later he stepped down onto the stern of the keelboat. The river craft settled underfoot, acknowledging the presence of the men. The door to the storage hold creaked open on its brass hinges. Dollard led the way down into the dimly lit interior. A single lamp trailing a fitful flame had been hung from the bow wall. It was enough to see by, and the two men placed the crate of rifles off to the side in order to keep the center of the cabin free and clear.

Out of the heart of the stillness rose a distant cry, sounding almost human, like a woman's shrill wail of terror. Both men recognized the howl of a she-wolf. And yet each sensed a chillness stealing through their veins, for the ancient wild call had a supernatural quality to it. And when it faded at last, the silence rushing in to take its place seemed overwhelming. "I know you," Dollard said. He leaned forward, his fists knuckling down into a pile of otter pelts. "And you ain't no wrangler."

Cole did not reply. He watched the scout carefully,

ever on his guard. If Dollard's hands dropped toward his holstered Colt, Anthem would lunge for him rather than try to beat the man to the draw.

"I know you," Dollard repeated. "Oh maybe not by name. I ain't sure if Anthem is your true handle or not. But it don't matter."

"Maybe the night's got you spooked, Sam," said Cole.

"In a pissant's eye it does. You've got me spooked. At least you did until I figured it out. Andy Morgan put her finger on it. She nailed your handle to the wall." Sam Dollard positively beamed in triumph. "You're the one they call Yellowboy. I should have known, when I first saw you use that carbine. You're a goddamn, bounty hunter!" Dollard stabbed a finger at the Texan. But the scout's grin faded as another realization dawned. "Why . . . you're after me. Ain't you?" Anthem only stared at the man. "Well, answer me. Answer me. You're trying to nail my hide. Answer, damn it."

Anthem stared and said nothing.

"Well, you can forget it. There's no papers hanging up on me in the territory. Not a one."

Cole thought of Glory and said nothing.

"What'd I ever do to you?" Dollard asked, backing away. But he kept his hands free of his gun. The boat was too close quarters for gunplay. "You're after me," Dollard repeated, nodding yet uncertain. Anthem's gaze continued to bore into the man. "Why don't you say something?"

Footsteps sounded on the deck and moments later

Andy Morgan climbed down into the cabin. She couldn't help but notice the tension emanating from the two men, especially the strained expression of the scout's face as he brushed past her and made his way to the bow.

Morgan was carrying a couple of burlap-wrapped quarters of salt meat, which she hung from hooks up toward the bow. She glanced over her shoulder as Dollard slipped away in the night. "Sorry if I broke anything up. You two looked like you were having a mighty exciting talk." She chuckled.

Cole shrugged and changed the subject. "You reckon the river's clear all the way down to Fort Conrad?"

"Depends on what you mean by clear," Andy replied. She took a pipe out of her pocket and lit it. She hooked one leg over a cracker barrel and rested a haunch on the lid. "Now, if you mean can we push off at first light? Yep. If you mean can we take this old boat of mine all the way down to Fort Conrad and not crack up on a chunk of ice or run aground or run her up onto the rocks . . . Shoot . . . well, that I can't say for sure." She blew a billowy cloud of tobacco smoke that hung in the air like a miniature thunderhead before eventually dissipating in the gloomy confines of the cabin. "You ain't exactly brought me the pick of the crop for a crew."

"Maybe you'd prefer Medicine Bear's Red Shields?"

"On the other hand, beggars can't be choosers," she conceded. She looked around the cabin with its plain, rough-surfaced walls, a scattering of three legged stools, and an assortment of barrels, crates, and piled pelts. It looked as if the woman had tried to load everything of value from her trading post onto the boat. Maybe she wasn't sure if she was coming back, thought Cole, his own doubts increasing.

"Valhalla," said Andy. "I give her that name. Met a drummer once who knew all about them Vikings, about how their ships sailed all around. Free as the wind they were." She took on a distant look, as if watching a scene long past unfold. "I guess that's the way I always tried to live, so it's only natural I'd be partial to such folks. They were eight feet tall and big and yellow-haired, sort of like you." Andy looked up at Anthem, who at six-foot-six towered over her. "Of course, you'd be a runt for a Viking," she added, putting him in his place. "And when they died, they burned their boats and set sail for Valhalla. That's Viking heaven, you know, where the men and women don't do nothing but eat, sleep, tumble in the sheets, and live free as the wind." She climbed off her perch and walked up to Cole. Andy lifted the brim of her hat and peered up at the man, pipe clenched firmly in her strong teeth.

"We're probably gonna need everyone who can carry a gun before we reach Fort Conrad."

"I know that," said Cole.

"Good," Andy replied, nodding. "Just wanted to be sure. I don't know what's between you and Dollard but I was hoping you wouldn't kill him before we make it downriver."

"I wouldn't think of it."

"You're a cold fish, ain't ya'."

"When I have to be."

The woman pursed her lips and then sighed. She took Anthem at his word. He was frank and honest and had fight in him, qualities she prized in a trail companion, qualities her husband, of long ago had lacked. It had been the death of him back along the Natchez Trace.

Cole studied the woman before him, her weathered features full of mischief. Square-shouldered, in an ankle-length woolen coat that made her seem solid and shapeless, she looked like a figure carved from a block of wood and not quite finished.

"What about you," Cole said. "Talk of carrying a gun: Are you depending on us men to do your fighting for you?"

"Now you've cut me to the quick," Andy Morgan exclaimed. "No man has ever done my fighting. Not even Mr. Morgan, may his poor cowardly soul find peace everlasting." The river woman opened her coat to display the worn grip of a Navy Colt tucked in the waistband of her dungarees and the sawed-off snout of a scattergun dangling from a leather shoulder strap along her side. Shells for the 12 gauge rattled in a coat pocket.

"I reckon things'll get close in and nasty afore they're done," she said with a wink and patted the shotgun. She turned around and lifted the lid of the cracker barrel, dug in among the crackers, and brought out a stick of dynamite. "And if push comes to shove,

I'll not have any red devil take my boat. I'll blow it to kingdom come first." She tucked the dynamite back into the barrel. Cole glimpsed several other sticks of explosives.

Captain Andy Morgan was prepared for war. But were the others? It was quite an army they had: a surveyor's assistant, a whore, a writer, a French vagabond, a crusty old Irishman, a cowardly scout, a bounty hunter, and a couple of gun-running brothers. With such an army arrayed against him, Medicine Bear would probably die laughing.

And that might be their only chance.

13

In the back room of the blockhouse, Silas Dean laboriously cleaned the round lenses of his eyeglasses with a soft kerchief. He sat on the edge of the bed and waited for Journey to come to him, to remove her clothes and stretch her sinewy body in naked splendor down beside him on the bed. He desired every coffee-colored curve of her, and felt every satin-smooth inch of her belonged to him. And none other. She was his passion. His desire was all-consuming.

Her hesitation made him frantic. What did she want of him? To make him jealous? Very well, then, he was jealous.

"Hurry up. The others will notice our absence before long," Silas said, urgency in his voice.

"I don't know," Journey replied, standing by the door.

"What kind of response is that?" Dean snapped.

"An honest one. After all, I'm an honest whore."

"Don't say that," Silas replied, his sensibilities offended. "Not while you are with me. Not ever again.

I'll take care of you. I am not without influence."

"You are a sweet boy. But what good is your money and influence here. Will you throw money at the Cheyenne? Will you order them not to kill you? They will kill you just the same." Journey folded her arms and tilted her head back and stared at the ceiling. Her black hair was unbound and hung down her shoulders. The lamp in the center of the room lent a sickly orange glow to the humble furnishings: a nightstand, ladderbacked chair and bed whose hand-hewed frame confined a mounded feather mattress.

"I followed you from Fort Conrad," Silas said with a wag of his head, enumerating a litany of what seemed to him an array of courtesies. "I paid you to stay with me. I saved you when the savages attacked."

"No. You did not save me. We just didn't get killed," Journey said. "Some live. Some die. I want to live. And we are not in San Francisco, we are not in St. Louis or any fine city. We are here. And you cannot help me here."

"Who can?" Dean said. "That colored up on the roof?"

"Maybe."

Silas searched her expression, hoping to discover the woman was toying with his emotions only to come at last into his arms. But what he read there dashed his dreams. He stood and walked around the bed to the shuttered window. He peered through the fireport at the black phalanx of pines arrayed against the blockhouse.

He fished in his coat pocket, removed a flask, and

emptied the last of the fiery contents down his throat. It burned all the way to his gullet and he embraced the pain.

"You're a whore," he said.

"Now we both know," she replied. She worked the latch on the door and stepped into the hall.

"So there I stood, alone, and at my back, the cliff, and before me, a dozen howling Prussians," DuToit exclaimed. His saber, glimmering in the lamplight, was held aloft in his right fist, ready to cut his imaginary enemy in twain.

"Will you be getting your story straight?" Danny McKane exclaimed. "First it was redskins, now it's Prussians."

"Cheyenne, then, if you will," DuToit conceded. He scowled and stared down his imaginary enemy. He took one step, then another, eyes wide, mustache bristling. "There was only one thing to do. I attacked. I cut them down, right, left, right." The saber sliced from side to side. DuToit, thrown off balance by the enthusiasm of his attack, stumbled over a chair and sprawled across the sergeant's table.

"An unseemly attack, DuToit," McKane said, standing. His trousers were spattered with spilled drink. He licked the whisky from his fingers and looked with obvious displeasure at the bottle the Frenchman had cracked. "There's trouble brewing this night. We'll have need of every man. Sober."

DuToit shoved himself upright and assumed an unsteady stance of attention.

"*Pardon moi,*" he said and hiccupped. He brought his saber up and tried to fit the tip of the blade into the scabbard, but his hands wavered and his red-rimmed eyes had trouble focusing. McKane reached out, steadied the blade, and slid the point into the scabbard's open end.

"Leave the mulekick be and stick to black coffee," the sergeant drily suggested.

"It's purely medicinal. I drink to forget," DuToit said.

"Forget what?" the sergeant asked.

DuToit almost confessed. He could no longer stand himself. But he hid his self-loathing and lied.

"I drink to forget the girls of the Boulevard Rochechonart. I drink to forget the friends of Montparnasse. I drink to forget the view from Notre Dame, the rooftops and the clouds, the Seine cutting like a scimitar through the heart of all I love. I drink to forget my Seine, my Bastille, my Paris."

"Maybe you'll return one day," McKane said, clapping the man on the shoulder. "Why, I might even go with you. Especially for the girls.'" The sergeant pounded the table top. "By heaven, I'll go. That is, if they like brave soldiers?"

"Brave soldiers," DuToit repeated, leaning forward. He reached for another bottle on the bar. "Ah, the perfect cure to a hopeless situation." And slid unconscious to the floor.

McKane sighed and shook his head in dismay.

"Is he hurt?" Journey asked from the shadows. She paused on the fringe of light, standing among the tables and countertops of the mercantile section of the room. She had tied her black hair back with a white bow.

"Won't know till we sober him up, Miss Journey," McKane said, touching the brim of his hat. "To my way of thinking, he feels fine now, though when he wakes up it'll feel like a siege gun firing in his head." The sergeant settled in his chair and propped his feet up on the table. "You better get some sleep, ma'am. Find you a bed somewhere."

"Oh, so that's what a bed is for," Journey coquettishly replied. The tone of voice didn't fit her features, which, though pretty, hardly radiated innocence. She headed for the ladder and started up to the roof. McKane watched her, taking pleasure in the way her firm derriere tightened and relaxed as she climbed. He wasn't so old or drunk or weary that he couldn't appreciate the woman. Or envy the man who waited on the roof above.

"You lonely?" Journey asked as her head poked through the roof. She climbed up through the opening and dropped the trapdoor into place as her legs swung clear. Then she walked across the roof to where Ben leaned his elbows on the split-rail wall. Like a Moor on some castle of old, the black man kept his vigil on the parapets of Morgan's Landing.

"Well?" she said.

Ben had to consider his response. He never felt more alone in his life, yet he reveled in being his own man. He'd done a lot of growing up the past few days.

"Lonely? No," he said, and his breath billowed on the night air. She drew close to him, drawn to his warmth. He handed her a blanket intended for himself. Since she was without a coat, he played the gallant.

"Good," said the mulatto. "I am tired of lonely men." She yawned and sat with her back to the wall. She tugged on his trouser leg, inviting him to snuggle next to her.

"Afraid I'll bite?" she asked. She lowered her eyes and gently laughed. "I haven't bitten a man in weeks."

He glanced out at the darkness. Her presence had certainly livened up what promised to be a boring few hours. Where was the harm?

He eased down alongside the woman. She worked herself into the crook of his arm.

"Ben Wheatley," she said, repeating his name. "What do you think of me, Ben Wheatley?" Her breath fanned his cheek as she spoke. Her eyes were wide and bright and glittering like ice-coated agates or black pearls and as impenetrable to his scrutiny.

" 'It seems she hangs upon the cheek of night like a rich jewel in an Ethiop's ear,' " he replied, choosing to quote from *Romeo and Juliet*.

"You talk funny," she giggled. "But I like what you say."

"It's all that matters," he said.

"I like the way you talk. I like the way you fight, too," the woman observed. "Rare to find both qualities together. Never known an Indian fighter to be educated."

"I'm hardly any sort of fighter," he scoffed.

"Take it lightly if you will, but I can read men as you can read books. A girl in my profession has to be able to or she could find herself in trouble. I watched you out in the meadow."

"I was petrified," he said. "I didn't know what I was doing." He tilted his head up and watched a cloud drift across the moon. He had killed a man today. He would remember this day for the rest of his life: the day he first took another man's life. He lowered his gaze from heaven to the rifle in his hands. He leaned over and propped it against the wall.

Odd. He missed the curious weight, the feel of blued steel and walnut stock. He tugged the revolver from his waistband. He was still familiarizing himself with its balance and heft.

"You liked it, didn't you?" she said, placing her lighter hand on his ebony wrist. "Standing when you should have run, looking death in the eye, the power of the gun. It woke something in you." She stroked the back of his hand and his fingers curled around the gun butt. "You enjoyed it."

"Maybe," he haltingly replied. Lord almighty, what magic was she working on him, what spell did she weave with her purring tone and warm, inticing touch. "Maybe," he repeated. "What does it mean?"

"You're learning," she said. "That if you're gonna play with the big dogs you gotta get off the porch." She brought his hand to her cheek, ran her tongue along his knuckles, then settled against him. "I'm not ever heading back East," she said. "Out here I can go as far as I want."

"If the Cheyenne will let you."

"That's where a special man comes in," she answered. She lowered his hand and placed it on her thigh. "One who's not afraid to leave the porch." She rested her head against his arm and with the wall at their back shielding them from the wind, she fell asleep.

Ben considered pulling away to resume his vigil, but he was drawn to her like a moth to the flame. And if she were dangerous, so much the better. He could handle it. Ben stared at the gun in his hand. He could handle anything.

Fractured lamplight seeped through shuttered windows of the blockhouse and streaked the trampled snow. Nothing stirred in the yard behind the house save the man walking back along the path from the keelboat. A broad-brimmed hat kept his features shaded from the meager light. But there was no mistaking Anthem, for only a few minutes had passed since Sam Dollard had left him in the keelboat.

As Dollard sighted on Anthem's rangy figure, he braced himself against the corner of the outhouse, settling the gun barrel in the crook of his thumb and the wooden wall. He waited patiently allowing the unsuspecting bounty hunter to draw within twenty-five feet of the outhouse.

Carefully now, Dollard cautioned himself. The first shot mustn't miss. Come on. Holding his breath, he cocked his revolver, and began to pull the trigger.

"Don't miss."

The voice so startled him he almost fired into the air. As it was he jumped back, slipped, and sat down in the snow.

Cole whirled, pulled his gun, and crouched low.

"Who the hell is it?" he called.

Sam hurriedly holstered his gun as the bounty hunter advanced along the rubble-strewn path to the outhouse. The door to the structure swung open.

"It's me, Zack Hammond," said the young man as he emerged from the upright little building. "Dollard's here, too. Waiting for me to finish."

Cole halted, slowly holstered his Colt beneath his coat and settled his gaze on the scout, who stood and dusted the snow from his rump.

"See you don't fall in, Sam," Cole muttered and cut across the yard to the blockhouse. The sound of his boots tramping over the ice-crusted snow was like that of brittle bones breaking, crack-crack-crack.

"Sonovabitch," Dollard growled.

Zack held his hands palm upward in a gesture of innocence. "I didn't aim to be sittin' in the middle of no gunfight."

"There wasn't gonna be any gunfight," Dollard scowled. "Just one shot."

"And if you missed? There I'd be, pants down and plumb pretty with a bullet hole in my naked ass." Zack finished buttoning his trousers. He watched as Cole disappeared inside the blockhouse. "I ain't got a whole lot of use for him, but he can sure use a rifle. And being as we're still in Cheyenne country . . ."

"Hell, those bucks today didn't have the stomach

for any more fight. And come morning we'll be safe on the river. Not even Medicine Bear will be able to touch us." Dollard spat in the snow, lowered his head, and glanced aside at the parfleche of gold Zack kept tied to his belt.

"You afraid to call Anthem out?" Zack said, swelling up with false courage. "A Hammond don't hold with back shooting. We meet trouble head on." The younger man assumed a cocky air. He crooked his thumbs in his belt, then patted the gun he had thrust in his waistband.

"Then you better get ready to meet it 'cause when we reach Fort Conrad, Anthem and McKane aim to see that gold of yours confiscated by the garrison commander."

Zack swung around, his mouth gaping and his expression at first wide-eyed in astonishment, turned narrow and mean.

"That's right," Dollard continued his lie. "I overheard him talking to that crazy old river woman. Even if they can't get you and your brother for gun running the Army can still lay claim to the gold your pa got for the rifles."

"Nobody's touching this," Zack said, patting the leather pouch. "I'll kill him."

"Head on? That will be something to see, younker," said the scout, grinning. "Of course, I'd be willing to help. For a share, say, a third."

"Go to hell," Zack snapped. He shivered and buttoned his coat.

"Split with me or split with the Army." Dollard

shrugged. He walked down the path, tucked his hands in his pockets, and began to whistle. He'd missed one opportunity, but planted the seed of another. The bounty hunter would not reach Fort Conrad alive.

"I ain't afraid of Cole Anthem," Hammond called. He glanced about at the darkness and hurried to catch up to the scout. "You hear me?"

"Sure . . . sure, Zack," Dollard replied. "Only it doesn't hurt to be careful. A man can't be too careful. Especially a rich man like you." He patted Hammond on the back and flashed his most encouraging smile.

"Well—uh—maybe we might could figure out some—uh—kind of split," Zack said. "As long as you figure we won't be running into any more of those damn Cheyenne."

"Trust me," said Dollard. "I know these savages."

14

The fire arrow hung in the air, spinning on its lethal course to thwack into the side of the blockhouse. Three more followed the first, stabbing the logs. Their pitch-smeared shafts fed on the timber, igniting the wall.

On the roof above, Ben Wheatley spun around at the sound, wondering at first what had caused it. Nearby, Journey muttered something unintelligible and pulled the heavy woolen blanket up to her chin.

Just out of Ben's sight, the arrows blackened and their shafts fell away, but not before the wall was aflame, timbers cracking and wood sap popping in the heat of the blaze. A gentle breeze sprang up, blowing out of the east and layering the smoke up over the edge of the roof.

Ben ran to the opposite wall and spied the tongues of lurid orange fire lapping the wall.

"Christ Almighty!" he exclaimed.

Another four arrows rose against the sky, burning in stark relief against the inky darkness. They hung poised as if suspended from invisible wires, then plunged earthward and buried their flaming warheads into the shingle roof.

He scrambled across to them, kicked one away, and smothered another in the blanket. Journey screamed, and he rolled up against the wall as five more arrows shot out of the night and missed him by inches. He straightened and emptied his Colt at a cluster of figures racing for cover. The warriors scattered as the bullets peppered the snow in their wake.

The fire was spreading and there was nothing anyone could do to stop it.

"C'mon," he shouted to Journey, who started toward the trapdoor.

Cole sat upright at the sound of the gunshots. It took a few moments for the sleep to clear from his eyes and for his mind to start assimilating his surroundings. He jumped to his feet, noticing that McKane, Dollard, and the others had also been alerted by the gunshots. They were scrambling out of their bedrolls and gathering their coats and guns.

Cole spied the serpentine tendrils of smoke drifting out of the hall leading to the back room, Andy Morgan's room. He grabbed up his carbine and coat, and rushed across the room at an awkward gait as he worked the stiffened muscles of his back.

"What the hell's going on?" McKane called out. The answer came as the trapdoor thumped open, and Journey and then Ben Wheatley scrambled down from the roof.

"Fire!" the black man shouted.

Cole had already plunged into the smoky depths of the hall. Crouching low, he reached the bedroom at the end of the passage and stepped inside. The back wall was ablaze and tongues of flame curled around the logs. Smoke blanketed the ceiling and partly obscured the interior. But he could make out enough to see the cot was empty. Nor was anyone by the hand-carved desk or washstand. So where was Andy Morgan? Cole backed, choking, into the wall and retraced his steps. Gunfire sounded in the front room as Silas Dean opened up on a shadow flying past the shuttered window. Cole ran into the room and headed toward the door at the rear of the blockhouse. McKane already seemed to know what to do and waved for the others to fall in behind Anthem.

"Head for the keelboat, she's our only chance," roared the sergeant.

Cole threw the door open. From out in the dark, the Sharps buffalo gun thundered and a head-sized chunk of the doorsill exploded in a shower of slivers. The impact of the bullet so close at hand sent Cole sprawling onto the path.

Behind him, McKane leaped out and leveled the Henry and loosed a couple of shots. Dollard darted through the doorway and fired at the shadows near the outhouse. Cole rising to one knee, brought the Winchester to bear and blasted away at the scattering silhouettes. Getting to his feet, he took off at a dead run toward the boat.

He spotted a brave racing along the riverbank. The

warrior swung a pair of lit lanterns stolen from the barn. It was obvious he intended to crash them against the hull of the keelboat.

Anthem fired and missed. Dollard and McKane fared no better as the brave dipped below the overhanging riverbank. The Cheyenne had to be stopped!

Arrows whirred toward the men, spinning across the firelit clearing. The blockhouse, nearly engulfed in flames, lit the surrounding clearing with a ghostly orange glow, making specters of the men strung out along the path.

Up ahead, the brave with the lanterns climbed up to the pier. Cole drew a bead on the warrior, held his breath, then exhaled and squeezed the trigger.

The hammer struck with an audible click. A defective cartridge.

"Shit!" Cole muttered.

A couple of Henry's boomed in unison and slugs ploughed furrows in the pier at the warrior's feet. The brave loosed a wild, animal cry and swung the lanterns in a circle over his head. Then from the ship's hold, the twin barrels of a double-barrelled game gun bellowed like a cannon. The lanterns shattered in the brave's grasp and doused him with oil. The impact of the pellets flung the warrior against the pine board rail. It cracked, broke in half, and the dying man tumbled like a burning rag doll into the icy waters of the Rogue.

That solved the mystery of Andy Morgan's whereabouts, Cole noted. She must have stayed down to guard her boat. Now she stood and waved to the men on the path, then reloaded the .12 gauge in her hands. She cursed the warriors lurking in the lessening dark and dared them to cross her path.

A long, high-pitched scream of pain brought Cole's attention back to the problems at hand. Silas Dean dropped his rifle and crumbled against Du Toit. The journalist clutched a feathered shaft jutting from his shoulder. He turned and Cole could see the rest of the arrow poking six inches out the back of his shoulder.

McKane worked his way over to the wounded man.

"Oh God, I'm dying," Dean exclaimed. "It hurts like hell. Oh, my God."

"If you think that hurts, wait'll you feel this," said McKane. He grabbed just behind the arrowhead and snapped the shaft in two. Silas shrieked. McKane, with the expertise of a man who had performed this task many times in his life, yanked the arrow out of the journalist's shoulder. Dean's eyes rolled up and he pitched forward. Du Toit, wide-eyed, his bloodless features drawn tight, ducked down and lifted the unconscious man onto his shoulder.

Cole ran up and blocked Sam Dollard and Zack Hammond from continuing down the path.

"Form a skirmish line," he ordered.

"We ain't in the goddamn army," Zack growled.

Cole didn't have time to argue. He jabbed the business end of his carbine into Hammond's chest.

"Stand with me or die here," Cole said, his features a mask of malevolent intention that Zack in no way wanted to face. The younger Hammond turned and began firing at two braves crouched near the barn.

"Want me to take the gold?" Jay Lee said, his breath rasping in his throat. He held out a bandaged hand and gasped in a lungful of air. His massive weight didn't make things any easier.

"Go on," Zack retorted. "I'm playing hero."

"But the gold?" Jay Lee protested. An arrow buried itself in the ground at his feet. "Forgit it," the fat man said and raced down the path.

Cole waved Ben Wheatley and Journey past him. Wheatley hesitated, wondering whether or not to remain at Anthem's side.

"Go on," Cole shouted. "Get the girl to the boat." He shoved Wheatley in the right direction. Back near the blockhouse, the big Sharps boomed. Cole winced despite himself and ducked.

"By the out back," Sam shouted and brought his Henry to bear, chasing High-Backed Wolf with his buffalo gun back behind cover. Another Cheyenne galloped around the corner of the blockhouse and, crouching low over the neck of his mount, notched an arrow to his bowstring. He had four more clenched in his teeth. He straightened to fire and Cole squeezed off a shot. The brave loosed his arrow toward the sky and rolled off the rump of his mount.

Cole glanced toward the boat and saw the others had gained the deck. Wheatley, McKane, and DuToit were already manning their poles. Andy Morgan was at the keel and motioned toward the three men who remained ashore.

"Let's get out of here," Cole shouted. He clapped Zack Hammond on the shoulder. Hammond needed no prompting. He spun around and scampered for the river. Dollard put another couple of rounds into the "necessary" to keep High-Backed Wolf's Sharps pinned down and then dashed after Zack.

Cole continued to back down the path, keeping both High-Backed Wolf and the braves by the barn from showing themselves. When he ejected the last shell from the Yellowboy, he whirled and leaped up to the dock and, keeping low as possible for a man his size, covered the remaining distance to the boat in three great strides.

"Welcome aboard," Andy shouted as Cole came aboard. To the pole men she cried, "Put your backs into it!"

DuToit, McKane, and Wheatley immediately began walking the length of the boat, determined to get the boat moving as quickly as possible. Cole took a pole off the top of the cabin and joined them. With DuToit on the port side, Anthem was exposed to the Cheyenne on the riverbank.

Jay Lee emerged from the cabin, alarmed that Zack, who had crawled to the bow up on deck, might have been left behind.

"Zack! Where's my brother, damn it?" he yelled.

Sam Dollard pointed toward the bow. Jay Lee pulled himself on top of the cabin and crawled forward on hands and knees as the keelboat nosed into the river.

"Zack, are you all right?"

"Don't worry, the gold's right here on my belt," Zack said, glancing up at his older brother. "Get back inside, you idiot," he added, searching the firelit shore and dancing shadows lining the riverbank. Suddenly a shadow froze, became a man, High-Backed Wolf brandishing Zack's own Sharps rifle.

The big gun boomed. Jay Lee Hammond was lifted bodily in the air and flung from the boat, trailing an arc of crimson and gray matter in his wake. He splashed into the river, floated for just a moment, and then sank before Wheatley could hook him with the pole.

"Son of a bitch," Zack muttered beneath his breath, staring at the spot where Jay Lee had been but a moment ago.

Colt revolvers and Henry rifles returned High-Backed Wolf's fire, but he wisely flattened himself beneath the reeds growing at the water's edge. The leader of the raiding party waited until the keelboat had drifted farther downriver before emerging from the bitter cold water. Then, using the Sharps for support, staggered up the riverbank. He knew what he had to do. Medicine Bear must be warned.

High-Backed Wolf had failed to secure the Henry repeaters. The *ve-ho-e* had escaped, at least for now. But he would ride his horses to death if need be to find the rest of the Red Shields. He turned to the Rogue River and the boat being carried on the current to safety. The brave lifted the rifle above his head and cried out in a voice of fury that carried down the hills.

Cole shouldered the pole and paused to listen as did everyone on the boat. From the hold, Silas Dean began to groan in pain. But no one paid him any mind. They

listened to the ghostly, high pitched wail carrying
across the water, following in ever fainter echoes that
reverberated along the shore, taunting and threatening.

They didn't need to understand the words High-
Backed Wolf cried to know what he said.

15

★

Medicine Bear swept down out of the hills at the head of his braves like a raging forest fire sweeping out of control and consuming everything in its path. They struck the trapper's camp in the predawn light even as Morgan's Landing was set afire, a two-day's ride away.

The site of the camp was a creek-fed meadow littered with felled timber, the roughly assembled outer walls of a cabin, and a couple of wagons loaded with pelts. The thirteen trappers had slept in tents, beneath wagons, or by their fires. Several were simply trampled to death, still struggling to free themselves from their bedrolls. There had been no warning. The lone sentry lay sprawled on the ice-patched ground, throat slashed and stone-cold dead.

One of the trappers, a big bear of a man, staggered out of his tent brandishing a pistol in one hand and a Bible in the other. Lances ripped his flesh and the hooves of the war ponies numbered his bones.

Medicine Bear rode through the encampment and

as he reached the edge of the clearing noted a line of braves watching him. He recognized an elder of the Red Shield Society, Sacred Horse, who waited at the head of his followers on the crest of a hill less than a hundred yards away. These Red Shields had come from deep in the heart of the mountains. Medicine Bear had hoped the elder Red Shields would come. He waved his spear toward them and rode from the battle. A glance over his shoulder told him the battle was over. His warriors were stripping the dead.

Medicine Bear rode up alongside Sacred Horse and greeted the older man with a great show of warmth.

"You ride well," Sacred Horse said. He was a short, thick man with silver streaking his long black braids. He wore the trappings of a Red Shield warrior, though his lance sported many eagle and raven feathers. He had brought twenty men with him from the high country.

"So you make war upon the *ve-ho-e*." Sacred Horse noted how the younger braves in the clearing below quarreled and fought among themselves over the spoils of their raid. Such conduct was shameful and undignified. These young men bothered him, perhaps their war chief most of all. He considered Medicine Bear rash and much too headstrong. Still, many of the younger men followed his example.

"As do the Lakota, the Mihniconju, the Tongue River Tribe, and those of Otter Creek," said Medicine Bear. "Soon we shall ride to where the tribes are gathering. But first we will win glory for ourselves that our words will carry weight in the great council to come."

"Perhaps you should have met with the council first before riding the war trail," Sacred Horse suggested.

"I do not need a bunch of old men to tell me how to fight!" Medicine Bear retorted. "Come with us or go your own way." He swung about and rode back the way he had come. The hooves of his mount sank deep in the soft earth.

Sacred Horse sighed. He glanced over his shoulder at the warriors watching him. The younger ones were eager to join the Red Shield braves below. Sacred Horse started forward. Against his better judgment he chose the path Medicine Bear had left for him to follow.

By midmorning the river had widened to a hundred feet across, fed by watery arteries carrying runoff from the snow-blanketed summits. Pines dotted the riverbank and snow-patched meadows revealed themselves beyond granite ridges as the keelboat passed among the mountains. It was a noisy passage with sheets of ice cracking and shattering underneath the boat's pointed bow. Often the current was not enough to propel them through the ice and brute force was needed. It was slow going.

"Use your backs," Andy Morgan shouted to the pole men. "Don't try to muscle your way through." Ben Wheatley stumbled and momentarily lost his balance. "Don't walk off the boat," she cautioned. "Keep the rhythm. Keep the rhythm."

On one side, Dollard and Zack Hammond paused to mutter curses at the boat, the river, and Andrea Morgan. She ignored their insults. Cole and Ben glared at the poles as if they were mortal enemies. Every man but Silas Dean, who was resting below, had blistered palms. Andy promised their skin would toughen and callus over before long. No one believed her.

So it was push and strain, walk the length of the boat, lift the poles out of the water, return to the bow, then thrust the poles into the rocky bottom, and repeat the process. Cole lasted another half hour before he relinquished his post to McKane. Then Anthem returned to the stern where Andy, on a raised platform so she could see over the cabin, guided the keelboat.

"You gonna need someone to spell you on the rudder?"

"Reckon not," the wiry old woman said, a clay pipe clenched between her teeth, the pungent aroma of tobacco pronounced here at the stern. "I know the Rogue. There's ice and sandbars and enough rocks to stove us in if we aren't careful. Better I handle this." She paused to holler at the men. "Watch the ice. Break it with your poles."

"I'm tryin' " Zack shouted. The keelboat shuddered and Hammond almost fell into the river before the sheet of ice cracked beneath the weight of the boat.

"DuToit's acting sort of queer," Andy said. "He even tried to order me around until I told him what he could do with his orderin'. I don't care what rank he held in the French army, I don't let any man tell me what to do."

She looked back the way they had come, where a dark smear against an otherwise clear azure sky pointed the way to the charred remains of the Landing, obscured now by a barrier of hills.

"I built that place with my two hands, Cole," the river woman said. "With no one around to help me but a couple of drunk trappers. I sure hate to see it go like that. A lot of hard years to end up a patch of smoke in a cold blue sky."

"Well, Andy, there's more than one spot for a landing along the Rogue."

"Not for me. I've done with the high country." She tucked a graying strand under her floppy-brimmed hat. Her expression was firm, utterly resolute.

Cole knew there was nothing he could do or say to console her.

"When do we get to rest?" called Zack as he shouldered the pole and drove one end down into the river.

"Save your breath for the job at hand," Cole replied. "You haven't been at it long enough to even start breathing hard." His hard gaze centered on Zack. "About time you did some honest work, anyways." Anthem disappeared down into the hold.

Morgan couldn't help but get her digs in. "Say, Zack, if'n the work's too hard for you, I can always bring us close in to the riverbank and you can walk the rest of the way to Fort Conrad."

"Shut up, you old witch. Shut up or I'll put an end

to you right here!" Zack snarled, his hand dropping to the gun at his side.

The fact she laughed in his face infuriated him further. She kept her left hand on the rudder, and with her right leveled her sawed-off shotgun directly at his belly. "You scare me about as much as your pa did, which is not at all."

Zack considered the possibilities. He did not like the looks of the .12 gauge. He sucked in his gut, shrugged, and started back to work, shouldering the pole and sauntering toward the bow.

Anthem made his way down the slippery steps and into the warm interior, where Journey fed wood to the small cast-iron stove near the bow. A coffeepot stood on the glowing top of the stove and filled the cabin with a welcome aroma. Silas Dean, his shoulder thoroughly cleaned and bandaged, lay on a bench seat built into the wall. His features were bunched and every time the keelboat jolted against a large sheet of ice, the journalist groaned.

On the opposite side of the boat, Philippe DuToit had fixed himself a command post of crates. He had spread a territorial map across the top of an improvised table, and was busily scanning it and making notes on the border or the map. He waved Anthem over to him.

"I have personally examined our situation," the Frenchman said. "As I am the only one here with any command experience, I have assumed leadership of this expedition."

Anthem stared at the man, uncertain exactly how to respond. He glanced at Journey, who shrugged and shook her head. Cole had seen men snap before, during the war. One moment they were fine, and the next second, in another world no man in his right mind could fathom.

"Maybe you ought to go up and take some air, DuToit," Anthem suggested.

"*Corporal* DuToit," the Frenchman corrected, bridling at such casual disregard for his station.

"Corporal DuToit," Anthem patiently acquiesced. He saw no reason to rile the poor man. "It might encourage the men to see you on deck."

"Mmm. *Mon dieu*, I think you are right." DuToit climbed off the crate of ammunition he had been using for a seat. "A fine idea, Mr. Anthem." He climbed the steps and disappeared through the doorway and out on deck, where he immediately began to harangue Andy Morgan for her slovenly appearance.

Cole chuckled and wondered how long it would take before Andy pitched him overboard. The bounty hunter continued on through the hold and paused beside Dean.

"He's asleep," Journey said.

"Doesn't look it," Anthem replied as the boat shuddered and the journalist winced and moaned softly.

She tapped a half full bottle of rye whiskey set on a shelf nearby. "I poured as much in him as I did on the wound," she matter-of-factly informed him. "Besides, he can't hold his liquor."

"You know him well," he drily observed.

"As much as I know any man," she coldly stated. She poured a cup of coffee.

"That for me?" he asked.

"It's for whoever wants it," she replied. Then looking him straight in the eye, she added, "Like me."

"Dean been around you long?"

"Couple of months."

"Nice fellow."

"Oh, shut up."

"Just being friendly, Journey," he said in a low voice.

"You got no call to be friendly or otherwise, Cole Anthem," she said, her voice a mixture of malice and bitterness.

"I thought we were friends."

Journey helped herself to a cup of coffee, sighed, looked up at him, and softened. "Maybe I'm just sick of men. And you certainly qualify." She studied him a moment. He met her scrutiny, his own gaze uncomplicated and frank. "Oh hell, I'm just so tired of being scared," Journey observed. Suddenly her gaze shifted and she looked past him to the man in the doorway.

"You got any coffee for a thirsty man?" Ben Wheatley asked. He descended into the hold and trailed the aroma of freshly boiled grounds to its source.

"Where's DuToit?" Cole asked. Footsteps sounded on the roof above and a moment later he had his answer as the Corporal began an enthusiastic rendition of the French national anthem. "Oh God," he muttered. He gulped down the contents of his cup and headed topside.

Ben glanced at the blue-enameled coffeepot. "Is there enough left for me?" he asked again.

"Why don't you pick it up and find out," Journey replied, moving toward him, a hint of a smile on her face. "Oh, your hands," she exclaimed, noticing the blistered flesh. She cupped his fingers and kissed the tender palms. "Poor baby," she purred.

He managed to swallow and finally worked his hands free of the grasp. "They'll be fine . . . uh, as soon as they toughen." He wriggled his fingers and winced. "I'll never play the piano again." He started to laugh, then thought about Doc Fleming, dead, and the comfortable life back in Boston that was closed to him now. "There's a lot of things I'll never do again," he ruefully added.

Without warning, the keelboat came to an abrupt stop as the bow dug into a sandbar. The coffeepot flew off the stove and spattered the back wall. Journey and Ben were knocked off balance and tumbled onto a stack of flour sacks that cushioned their fall as the keelboat canted slightly to starboard. Wheatley and the mulatto landed in a tangle of arms and legs. She struggled halfheartedly against the man lying atop her. Ben heard footsteps and shouts coming from on deck.

"If you two are gonna bundle, why don't you do it outside?" Silas said in a voice thick with jealousy and pain. He swung his legs off the bunk and sat up. His features were pale, almost bloodless, and the flesh was drawn tightly over his skull. His jaw was rigid, teeth clenched.

Ben stood and helped the mulatto to her feet. "I'm sorry, ma'am."

"Accidents will happen. Again, soon, I hope," she replied, smiling provocatively.

He turned and started to leave. He paused by Silas and stared at the wounded man for a moment. Dean was the first to look away. The black man continued on up the steps.

On deck Andy was shouting orders to the men at the bow, who were gradually poling the keelboat back off the bar upon which she had unwittingly steered. DuToit was huddled, shivering on deck, his clothes soaked. The jolt had thrown him from the roof into the frigid river. Sergeant Danny McKane, from the look of his bedraggled uniform, had fished the Frenchman out of the shallows and back to the keelboat.

"The crazy witch just about wrecked us," Zack complained to the men around him, who paid him no mind. Dollard set his pole aside while Cole took a stout hemp rope already tied to the bow and leaped onto the bar.

"C'mon," he called to Sam, and the scout shrugged and did as he was told. The men sloshed through the shallows, cracking translucent sheets of ice as they headed for the riverbank.

Morgan hurried to the bow, untied the rope, and trotted back to the stern, where she secured it through an iron ring. She glanced at Ben.

"Take you a Henry and climb up on the cabin. Watch those boys and if you see any Red Shields, don't miss."

McKane hurried along to join Zack at the bow.

"Who's in command of this infernal vessel?" DuToit blurted. "I demand an inquiry." He began to shiver violently just as Journey appeared, recognized his condition, and lead him down into the hold to dry out.

"Now all we need is for some of them damned Cheyenne to show up," grunted Sam as he and Cole leaned into the rope. The forest surrounding them seemed devoid of life. The silence was ominous. "Shut up and pull," Anthem grunted. "On the count of three." His muscles rippled beneath his shirt, his boot heels dug into the soft earth. The rope cut into his shoulder blade as he leaned into it. "One-two-three." His voice barely carried to the line of trees, where the emerald gloom swallowed their voices.

The two men pulled together. Dollard, though smaller by half a foot, was solidly built. And with the help of the men on the bow, who shoved with all their might as soon as the line grew taut, the keelboat, like some crippled behemoth, waddled off the sandbar, retreating inch by inch from its course of folly.

Gradually Andy turned the bow toward the center of the river, where the current threatened to carry the boat downstream and strand Anthem and Dollard on shore. But she pitched a makeshift anchor on a short line that hooked into the bar and held the boat in place long enough for the scout and the bounty hunter to cross the sandbar to the keelboat. Cole, the last to board, waved to Andy, who brushed a wisp of silvery hair out of her face and hauled in the anchor.

The four men sank onto the runway, their backs to the hold as the keelboat, under Morgan's guidance, left the sandbar behind.

"The river's a woman," she said from the raised platform on the stern. "Every now and then she changes her ways, throws up a snag where she used to be clear going."

"Sure, and I'm glad we're headin' downstream. I've no love for this work," McKane managed to gasp. "I'll take forty miles a day on beans and a nag any day of the week."

"We'll reach Fort Conrad quicker if everyone helps," Andy called. She drew out her pipe and stuck it into her mouth, then relit the tobacco. She glanced past her cupped hands and flaring match, and watched as the men grudgingly stood and took their places along the runway, manning their poles.

The sun continued its descent toward the western mountaintops, the snowcapped peaks turning burnished gold. And all around, the land lay still and fair, the chill of the air lessened by the warmth of the sun.

They might just make it Cole thought to himself, that is, if they didn't get killed. Medicine Bear was out there somewhere. He wanted the keelboat and the rifles and ammunition. He wanted them bad.

By sundown Andy had steered near shore. The boat was secured with both anchor and a line run to a spruce growing near the river's edge. Back among the trees, McKane built a fire and Journey proceeded to fry some pork and bake a skilletful of biscuits she served up with a gravy made from the drippings and thickened with flour.

Cole Anthem and the rest lost no time in gathering around to be ladled out a portion of good, hot food washed down with strong black coffee.

After dinner, Cole cradled his Yellowboy in the crook of his arm. Setting his plate and cup aside, he walked from the campfire and began a final circle of the campsite before turning in. He wanted to make certain the area was secure before bedding down. He moved as quietly as a shadow through the stand of conifers. He halted, paused to listen, then hearing nothing resumed his patrol. He kept his mind clear now. Every sense must be alert. Much of the snow had melted during the daylight hours. Now with the mantle of night draped upon the land, the remaining patches slowly became glazed with ice.

Cole finished his circuit a hundred feet upriver and followed the undulating bank back toward the campfire, which glowed like a beacon against a lofty black backdrop of lodgepole pine and spruce towering into the deep-blue velvet sky.

A soft breeze was up and an occasional cloud scudded across the sky. McKane stood by the river's edge, a cup of steaming coffee in his hand. He turned as Cole approached. The two friends stood side by side and looked into the night. Cole shivered in spite of himself. It wasn't all that cold, at least not as it had been. He scratched the sandy stubble covering his cheek. McKane sipped his coffee. His woolen coat was unbuttoned and his battered campaign hat tilted back off his forehead. He gulped the last of his coffee.

"I never knew a whore yet what couldn't make a good coffee," McKane observed. The jaunty little Irishman squatted and washed out his cup. "Mother Mary, but did you hear that." He pointed toward the boat, tethered about thirty feet from shore. Here in the bend of the river the shallows stretched out from shore almost to the boat. "There, see!"

Something splashed in the water near the boat. "Trout." The sergeant said the word with such deep reverence only another fisherman could understand.

"Good eating," Cole mentioned.

"Best in the world," the sergeant chuckled. "Give me a plate of panfried trout and a bottle of aged Irish whisky and I'll die a happy man." He slapped his thigh. "By God, when these hostiles are put down, I'm coming back here, this very spot, and catch me that fish." He dug a slim hard cigar out of his pocket, a tight smile on his weatherbeaten face.

"They're Busby's special order. DuToit took 'em off the major's body. Figured he wouldn't mind." McKane held up his hands in mock innocence. "The crime would be in letting them go to waste." He tucked the cigar in the corner of his mouth and started back to camp. He had first watch and another cup of coffee would see him through.

*   *   *

Zack was unable to take his eyes off Journey. He reckoned he was handsome enough and he had some gold, too. He couldn't figure out why she hadn't come to him. He stretched out in his bedroll and fancied how it would be with her. The way she moved, the way her lithe form filled the man's clothing she wore. He bit his lower lip and pondered just how he might be able to catch her alone. He hadn't given Jay Lee a single remorseful thought.

Sam Dollard and Silas Dean faced one another over a deck of cards. A flat stub of granite served as a table. Bullets were chips and five-card stud the game.

"Three treys," Dollard said in good humor.

Silas scowled and tossed in his two pairs, jacks and nines. "Never seen such luck."

"Luck, hah," Dollard said. "Skill helps. Cheating, too."

"What?" Dean blurted.

"Don't look so shocked," said the scout. "Everybody cheats. It's one of the rules." He shuffled the cards and dealt another hand. Dean continued to scowl.

"Aw, c'mon," Dollard said, patting the younger man on the shoulder. "You can cheat, too, if you want. All right?" He nodded as if answering for Silas and opened with a bet of five cartridges.

"We are traveling with some bad company," DuToit said in a gloomy voice. He stood by the fire, warming his backside. He searched the faces of the people around him, then lifted a canteen to his lips, and drank deep until a hand snatched it away. Cole sniffed the contents and wrinkled his nose. Cheap whiskey.

"We may all be dead tomorrow," DuToit said to him.

"Then that is the way the hand's been dealt," Cole said, leading DuToit to the Frenchman's bedroll.

"Shut him up or I will," Zack shouted.

"I say we'll get to Fort Conrad," said Andy. "Don't worry, Philippe, we will make it. There's more'n fifty men stationed there. Not to mention all the trappers and prospectors and townsfolk. Yessir, I'll buy you a whole bottle of whiskey from the sutler's store when we all do, so you won't feel so bad about not dying a heroic death."

"It'll be a cold day in hell when you buy me a whole bottle, Andrea Morgan," said DuToit. He stretched out on his blanket, lay back, and almost immediately began to snore.

Ben Wheatley studied the man through the dancing flames. The Frenchman had begun to set his nerves on edge. When Cole came around and lay down on the blanket nearby, Ben voiced his concerns in a low voice.

"You reckon we've had it, Cole?"

The Texan tucked an arm behind his head and stared up at the stars. He drew his Colt, held it in his right hand, and lay still. Ben thought he'd gone to sleep when Anthem answered him, quoting a line Wheatley recognized from *Hamlet*.

" 'If it be not now, yet it will come: the readiness is all.' " Cole rose and met Ben's intrigued stare. "I have read a book or two in my time." He settled back and closed his eyes, tilting his hat down over his face.

Ben nodded. He looked around him, at the men and women in a circle around the fire.

"The readiness is all," he whispered. He lay back and tried to rest, his rifle close at hand.

16

Journey walked from the clearing. She stepped around the place Silas had prepared for her beside him on the ground. Though his buffalo robe was large enough for two, she had no intention of lying with him. Journey moved out of the circle of fire-light and headed down to the river, led by the sweet music of the rushing current. The night was clear and cool, not bitter as it had been, and she was grateful for the opportunity to be alone, to be away from the company of so many men, and to have the moon and stars all to herself.

She reached the river's edge and followed the bank upstream several yards until she crossed a hillock bound on three sides by the river and soft with ferns and wild grasses. There, hidden from view, she unbuttoned her shirt and, kneeling at the water's edge, dipped a kerchief into the cold water and proceeded to wash several days' worth of grime from her face, neck, and upper torso. Though the water was bracing and took her breath away, it left her wonderfully invigorated. She spread a blanket upon the spring rushes and lay back to stare up at the stars. The world was quiet, save for the river, and lay at peace.

At times, Journey's past was but a distant memory, and she could allow herself to feel pure and sweet as a new bud and virginal as a white cloud drifting on the wind. She closed her eyes and tried to remember a prayer her mother had taught her long ago before she had been sold to a brothel owner in Little Rock, Arkansas. There had been prayers in her life once, but she had been a mere toddler then. Now when she closed her eyes, instead of picturing the mother who bore her, Journey could only create an image of herself at eleven being led into a room. There had been a man there, a big man who had fussed over her and dressed her up in girlish finery and then carried her to bed. . . . She covered her face with her hands and tried to drive the image from her mind. The memory faded, though the pain lingered, and she was on the riverbank again, listening to the lap of water wearing down the rocks.

Journey envied the Rogue and its ability to obliterate the debris of life's storms and floods. She wished it were that easy for a person to cut loose of painful memories. She wanted to be rid of the past. How grand, to be able to begin anew with none of the hurts and horrors of yesterday.

She uncovered her face and looked up into the leering, hungry visage of Zack Hammond. For a moment she thought she had imagined it. But then he dropped on her, pinning her shoulders to the ground with his knees and gagging her with his bandanna.

She freed her hands and tried to shove him off. He caught her wrists and forced them back above her head. Then he slowly worked his weight along her chest until he could bring his lips to her cheek and neck. She arched her back, twisted in his grasp, and tried to knee him, but he moved with her and avoided the injury. He covered one of her dark nipples with his mouth and tongued the flesh until it hardened. Then he rose and brought his face to hers.

"I've been watching you. I like what I see." He shook his head in an unspoken word of caution. "Now, now, now. I ain't gonna do anything to you that ain't been done before. Only difference is I'm a better class of man then you're used to. I got me some gold and it's all for me now that my dumbass brother got hisself killed." He licked her neck and ran his tongue over her cheek and chin. "You gotta sweet taste, little nigger gal, a sweet, sweet taste. Be good to me and maybe some of my gold will find its way into your pocket." With a mighty shove, her strength magnified by her rage, she unseated him and scrambled to her feet and ran toward the camp. She yanked the bandanna away and began to shout, but he caught up to her and dragged her down once more.

"No," she shouted. "NO!"

His hands clawed her trousers and in so doing left himself unprotected. Her talons raked his cheek, drawing blood. He howled and fell back, clasping a hand to the crimson furrows disfiguring his features.

"You bitch!" He dove and trapped her legs as she struggled to stand and pulled her back down the hillock almost to the river's edge. She lunged at him like a wildcat. He rapped her along the side of the head with his Colt, and the woman staggered and fell to her knees. Zack shoved Journey onto her backside and ripped away her shirt and started on her trousers, fighting the buttons and belt in his haste to mount her. He didn't see Ben Wheatley moving in until it was too late.

Wheatley arrived at a dead run and barreled into Hammond, and the two men landed together in the water. The rushing cold killed any desire Zack had and he staggered out of the shallows, sputtering and shaking the water from his clothes. His hair was matted to his skull. His cheek still hurt like hell.

Ben gasped for air and crawled to Journey's side. The plunge into the Rogue had been a sobering experience. She saw him coming toward her and panicked and tried to fight off what she assumed was another attacker.

"It's me," Ben shouted and caught her hands and dragged the woman to her feet. "It's Ben Wheatley."

Her eyes widened with recognition. "Oh Ben, he . . ."

"I know," he interrupted. "But I won't let him hurt you."

She stared past him and a look of alarm flashed across her features. Her expression was unmistakable, a desperate warning. Ben spun on his heels to face Zack, who rose from the greasy bank like an uncoiled spring, his right arm raised and in his grasp a bone-handled skinning knife. Without a sound the arm swept down. Ben, defenseless against the blade, shielded Journey with his own wiry frame. He would remember the moment to his dying day and in his dreams often relived each second in slow motion.

Zack's arm outstretched, the whisper of cold steel slicing the night air, and no way to escape the weapon, no way to leap out of harm's way without risking the life of the woman behind him. A fraction of a second was all that passed. One moment Ben Wheatley was a dead man and the next, the knife exploded in midair and the sharp crackle of a carbine reverberated along the river.

Standing atop the hillock, Cole Tyler Anthem levered another round into the chamber of his carbine and, holding the Winchester in his right hand, rested the rifle butt on his thigh, the barrel pointed toward the sky. He kept his finger on the trigger.

Zack watched the shattered knife plop into the river. He looked up at Cole. Hammond knew one wrong move on his part meant a bullet in the brisket. He smiled his broadest, friendliest smile. "Much obliged, Mr. Anthem. I reckon I lost my temper there. Glad you kept me from doing something I'd have regretted." He lifted his shirt to better reveal in the moonlight that he was unarmed.

"I'm always glad to do a good turn," Anthem replied. Behind him, Sam Dollard, McKane, and Andy Morgan were all on their way up from camp. Even Philippe DuToit came to see what the commotion was all about.

"No darkie lays a hand on Zack Hammond and gets

away with it. This ain't finished yet," Hammond
threatened, stabbing a finger at Wheatley. He turned
to leave, but Cole leveled his carbine at the departing
young man. Zack halted and stared at the Yellowboy
and the man who held him under the gun.

"Finish it," Cole said.

"Huh?"

"Finish it."

Cole nodded toward Ben, who stepped forward, the
anger welling in his breast.

"Yeah. Finish it, Zack," Ben said. He no longer
sounded educated, no longer a man of reserve and
culture. A boy's facade had shattered, revealing in its
place the face of a man, with a man's anger and a
man's pride.

Zack grinned and started toward Wheatley. Hammond closed in quick, cocked his fist, and Wheatley
hit him on the jaw with a hard left followed by three
vicious jabs to the belly that backed Hammond up. He
tripped over his own feet and fell down.

It was obvious Wheatley had studied the manly art
of fisticuffs. Hammond shoved himself erect; Ben
darted in and hit him with a couple of lefts to the side
of the jaw. Zack reeled, fell to his knees, and dropped
forward. Blood dripped from his split lips, from his
raked cheek. And worse than the pain, the black bastard was shaming him. He could hear Andy Morgan's
taunts. The sergeant whooped and hollered. And Sam
Dollard appeared to be enjoying the whole affair.

Ben looked up at Cole, shrugged, and dropped his
guard, figuring he had won the fight.

"No Marquis of Queensberry rules here," Cole shouted to Ben. Zack drew his legs up, crouched on the balls of his feet, like a wild animal ready to pounce.

Ben waved to Cole, he wasn't worried. He should have been. Hammond leaped up and hurled a fistful of wet sand in Ben's face, blinding the black man. Zack lowered his shoulder and buried it in Wheatley's stomach. The two men rolled to the ground. Hammond shot to his feet and aimed a vicious kick at Wheatley's head. The boot narrowly missed its mark, glancing off the black man's neck. Ben rolled along the grass, lessening the effect of the kick. He struggled to his knees and as Zack closed in, fell forward and wrapped his arms around Zack's legs, twisted, and threw Zack over his shoulder. Hammond rolled down the incline and landed in the shallows once again. Wheatley continued to struggle for air.

Zack clawed his way out of the water, sputtering and livid with rage. Journey lunged at him tooth and nail, but the man was stronger and quickly shoved her aside. Still, she had bought Wheatley enough time to catch his breath, and when Zack moved in, Ben had his wind again, though his eyes were still smeared with mud.

Hammond hit him in the belly and clubbed him along the side of his head. Ben staggered back, turned, and ran upriver along the shore, angling toward camp. Zack roared in triumph and gave chase.

"C'mon, you little rabbit, I'm a man for you, by heaven," Zack shouted. "I ain't done with you yet."

Ben ignored him and continued to wipe his water-soaked sleeve across his eyes until at last his vision cleared. Then he pretended to trip and lose his balance to allow Zack to gain on him. Hammond loosed a wild war whoop, barreled forward for the kill, and was completely caught by surprise when Ben whirled around and sent a hard right fist square into his face. Blood squirted, bones broke, and Hammond sat down and howled in pain at his poor broken nose.

Ben waited, fists ready, feet firmly planted. The running had ended.

Hammond, tears streaming from his eyes, stared up at Ben. A growl started deep in Zack's throat and became a cry of pain and outrage. "Oh, you bastard, you bastard!" Zack seemed to erupt from the ground and his fists pummeled and battered Ben's forearms, for the black man blocked every blow and held his ground, waiting for Zack to spend his energy. At last Hammond staggered back, arms limp and gasping for breath. He was furious that he hadn't done any damage to Ben. And with exhaustion and failure came the sickening revelation that he was probably in for the beating of his life.

Ben moved closer. Hammond tried to raise his weary arms to ward off the inevitable. Ben swatted aside the beaten man's defenses and caught him by the scruff of the neck. He dragged the hapless fool back to Journey, who had covered her torn shirt with McKane's military tunic. She glared at Zack's battered features. He wouldn't meet her gaze.

"Apologize," Ben said.

Hammond said nothing at first. Then Ben tightened his hold, shook the man, and drew back a fist.

"Sorry," Hammond managed to say through his swollen lips. Blood seeped from his flattened nose and dripped from his chin and stained his woolen shirt.

Ben released his hold. He seemed to notice for the first time the audience who had gathered to watch the fight. Cole and Sam Dollard, DuToit, Sergeant Mc-Kane, and Andy Morgan, westerners all. Ben had the distinct impression he had passed some sort of rite of passage. It had been unintentional. He'd acted on the spur of the moment in coming to Journey's rescue. And yet, he sensed an acceptance that had not been there before, despite the friendship men like Cole and McKane had shown him.

As he led Journey away from the river, he paused in front of Cole. "Thanks." He could still hear that knife slicing toward him.

"It was a lucky shot," Cole replied.

"I doubt that," Ben said, scrutinizing the man.

"Luck had nothing to do with it," Dollard interjected. "Not for a man in his line of work. You've had plenty of practice bringing men under your gun sights, haven't you, bounty hunter." Everyone looked toward Cole. "That's right, a bounty hunter. He's nothing more than a killer the law pays to do its dirty work. Most folks know him as Yellowboy."

"I knew you weren't no wrangler," McKane said, slapping his thigh.

"You after anybody in particular?" Andy Morgan

asked, eyeing Cole suspiciously. Her grip tightened on the shotgun cradled in her arms.

"Me," Sam Dollard spoke up. "But I can't figure why." His features hardened, his eyes narrowed and radiated menace.

"Glory Doolin," Cole said.

The blood drained from Dollard's face. "She was a friend of yours?" His Adam's apple bobbed as he gulped.

"Still is," Cole said. "She's alive, no thanks to you."

"She came looking for me. The bitch got what she deserved," Dollard said in a desperate voice.

"So will you," said Cole.

A scream ended the conversation, a cry of terror that rose in pitch and then as abruptly ended.

Cole broke into a run, his long-legged strides eating the distance. He already knew he was too late. But he had to try.

17

★

Blood still spurted from Silas Dean's slashed throat, but his killer was nowhere to be seen. The journalist was sprawled facedown, his head twisted to the side, arms outstretched as if he were trying to fly. He was almost completely out of his bedroll and close enough to the fire for one trouser leg to be singed.

"Damn," Andy Morgan remarked, kneeling by the dead man. "See here, he's been stabbed in the back, too. Lucky for us he left his rifle on the boat or there'd be a few more of us joining him."

Cole had his back to the corpse by the fire and stood outside the circle of light, his eyes searching the forest.

"We better pull out of here, Andy," he said. Morgan straightened and wearily stood.

"I'm thinking the same thing, Cole," the river woman said.

"First, of course, we will bury this poor unfortunate lad," Philippe DuToit spoke up. "I insist." He tilted his canteen and took a long pull. McKane crossed to the Frenchman and snatched the canteen away.

"Enough," the sergeant told him. He corked the canteen and draped it from his own shoulder.

"Sir, you will return that canteen or place yourself under arrest for insubordination."

"As soon as we reach Fort Conrad," the feisty little Irishman replied. "And the stockade there will be sweet to me as my blessed mother's arms. And as safe, you mark my words."

Dollard and Zack Hammond approached the campsite, and both of the men stiffened at the sight of Silas Dean. Dollard immediately spun around and trained his Henry rifle on the shadowy forest. By firelight Zack looked even more battered, his cheek ridged with drying blood. The bridge of his nose was flattened and a sickly white. Hammond stepped next to Dean, stared at the dead man and then shrugged. The easterner meant nothing to him.

Journey glanced at Hammond and took satisfaction at the sight of his ruined visage. She helped Andy and the sergeant quickly gather the supplies they had brought ashore. The task took but a few minutes, but that seemed an eternity to the men on guard who expected a war party to come whooping and howling out of the woods any second. Journey took a moment to kneel by Silas. She touched his shoulder and tried to remember a prayer, something to say for him. Despite DuToit's insistence, no one had made a move to bury the journalist. Journey was pragmatic enough to understand why. All their lives were in danger the longer they remained on shore. Still, she thought a few words would make it right, leaving him like this, food for the wolves.

All she could think of was something she had remembered as a child and never forgotten. "Now I lay me down to sleep, I pray the Lord my soul to keep . . ."

She stood, realized that Ben was nearby. He placed his hand on her arm. His expression revealed that he shared her sorrow. She wondered if he really understood.

"I didn't love him. I liked him when he was gentle, when he was full of dreams and would tell them to me. And I'm sorry he's dead. It makes me sad when dreams don't come true." Journey scooped up a handful of dirt and sprinkled it the length of the dead man's body.

Ben tugged her sleeve, "We better join the others. It isn't safe here."

Journey looked around and saw that DuToit, Morgan, and the sergeant were already halfway to the boat. Zack Hammond wasn't far behind.

"It isn't safe anywhere," she said. The woman sighed and fell into step alongside Wheatley. Cole and the scout were the last to leave the clearing, their rifles trained on the forest.

"What the hell was that?" Dollard said, swerving the Henry to cover a peculiar-looking clump of foliage. The brush shook again and an owl fluttered from the bush and alighted on the branches of a nearby spruce.

"Take it easy," Cole cautioned. He didn't like to

admit to being as alarmed as Dollard, but finding
Dean's freshly killed corpse had wrecked his nerves
as well. And he cursed his own stupidity. He had been
the last to scout the surrounding forest and had seen
no sign of an enemy. It was a damaging blow to his
confidence. A man in his line of work did not live
long by being careless.

The keelboat lay about thirty feet out in the river,
held only by an anchor now as Andy had untied the
line to shore. The boat was slowly drifting to midriver,
propelled by the current. Cole sucked in his breath as
the water reached above his boots and crept up to his
knees. His belly and groin tightened. The ice here had
already cracked and floated in loose, thin sheets on the
surface of the running current. His boots dug into the
gravel river bottom as he tried to hurry. Cole glanced
toward the boat, saw that Ben and the mulatto were
just being helped aboard, noticed Andy Morgan standing at the stern, working the keel now and bringing
the boat back in line.

Cole turned his back on the clearing and continued
on in earnest through the bitterly cold water toward
the boat, now about twenty feet away. Dollard, being
a smaller man, cursed as the current rose to mid-thigh,
but his thick, solid frame carried him forward. He
wasn't about to turn back.

The land seemed strangely devoid of life, as if it
had died with Silas Dean. The steady rush of the river
itself was muted. The effect was unnatural and ominous. Cole sensed the presence of death, poised, ready
to strike. But from which direction? Nothing stirred

onshore and he and Dollard were alone in the river.
Alone . . .

For the first time Cole noticed a rather peculiar phe-
nomenon. A reed poking six inches above the surface
of the river; no, two reeds there in a moonlit patch of
the river, like black straws thrust out of the silvery
surface and moving upstream against the current.

He slapped the rifle to his shoulder and fired, the
straw exploded, cut off just below the waterline. Cole
continued to fire, and as the Red Shield warrior
emerged from the waterline he stood up in the path of
a .44-caliber slug. The brave was slammed back into
the river on impact. Cole shifted his aim and blasted
the area around the second reed as it disappeared into
the shadows close at hand. Sam Dollard reached the
boat and McKane pulled him to safety. Ben grabbed
the man's Henry and ran to the bow and began pep-
pering the spot Cole had centered on.

A brave shot out of the river behind Cole and
whooped in triumph, his knife slashing down. Anthem
whirled and parried the knife thrust with the barrel of
the carbine. He swung the stock and cracked it against
the warrior's side. Ribs broke and the Cheyenne
gasped and staggered back. Cole tried to work the
lever of the carbine, but it had jammed and the stock
was shattered.

The Cheyenne gave a feral growl and leaped at
Cole. The bounty hunter glimpsed twelve inches of
jagged steel in the warrior's fist. He shifted the carbine
to his left hand, drew his Colt, and fired in a single
fluid motion. The brave splashed into the river a yard

away. Cole spun about, revolver cocked. A third brave floated facedown near the keelboat.

Cole waded the remaining distance to the boat. He moved as quickly as the footing would allow. McKane and Ben dragged him aboard. The bounty hunter sat on the runway and massaged his legs. McKane passed him DuToit's canteen. He uncorked it and poured some of its fiery contents down his throat. He didn't stop until he could feel his legs and tears sprang from his eyes.

By noon of the following day, the keelboat was making good time. Too good, Cole thought, as the shallow-draught boat pitched from side to side. The Rogue dropped several hundred feet here between two ridges that rose up to either side like granite forts. The river seemed to boil and churned itself to a frothy white as it rushed down what Andy Morgan call "the chute."

Cole had walked back toward the stern and stood alongside Morgan, who kept her leathery hands on the tiller. Cole blew into his hands. "You sure get the wind here. Christ, I don't know which is colder, me or this goddamn river," he managed to say through his chattering teeth.

McKane, Wheatley, and Sam Dollard were all on deck, their poles ready to ward off a collision with one of the granite boulders jutting from the riverbed. The boat pitched and bucked crazily in the current. The channel narrowed and the men had to struggle to keep from being thrown overboard. The boat entered the cleft between the great gray battlements of stone.

"Watch them cliffs, now," Andy called. "Young braves like to take pot shots at me from time to time. It's their idea of a fun way to scare somebody. Only the way things are these days I don't believe they'd be funnin'."

Anthem glanced up. It was a perfect place, all right. But he wasn't all that sure what he could do about an ambush under these circumstances. He was confident of his prowess with a rifle or belly gun, he trusted his skills, yet he doubted his ability to hit anything from the keelboat's careening deck. Nevertheless he scoured the cliffs for any sign of life.

The sun rode high in the cloudless cobalt-blue expanse of the sky. The temperature had risen enough to completely break up the ice at the lower elevations. As for the chute, the river never froze here.

With the sun on her once pretty face and the wind at her back, Andy was optimistic once again. "We'll be pulling safe and sound into Fort Conrad by late tomorrow afternoon, I reckon," she shouted. She hauled to the left on the tiller, and the keelboat glanced off a smooth, worn ton of granite. "That is, if we don't crack up."

The boat jerked viciously to the left, knocking the three men at the bow to their knees. McKane narrowly missed being thrown into the rapids.

"Shit! I hate this!" he bellowed.

"Thataboy, Irish," Morgan called out. "Keep us off'n them rocks."

At the bow, Wheatley dragged McKane to his feet.

The two of them jammed their poles into another boulder and, with fate's cooperation, managed to avoid disaster.

Andy was in her element now. She had run the chute many times in the past. A sense of exhilaration replaced the tension and gloom of the evening before.

"Anthem," Morgan shouted. "I need you now! Help me to hold her steady."

Cole leaped up opposite the river woman and added his strength to the tiller. The boat seemed alive to his touch; he could feel every tremor, every wrenching shudder the wood endured.

As for Morgan, it no longer mattered that her back and legs had begun to ache from the constantly alternating pressure. Or that her shoulders burned as if someone was twisting them out of their sockets. The boat had indeed become a wild, bucking animal whose every lurch threatened to drive them to disaster. But she had tamed the Rogue before and she would tame it now. "Hold on! Here we go!"

Twenty turbulent yards, then ten and suddenly the men at the bow were thrown to the deck as the boat nosed under the water and shuddered. Poles snapped with a loud report heard over the shouts of the men and the roar of the water. Then the boat heaved itself back up through the icy waters and was through the gorge and free of white water.

Morgan slapped Cole on the shoulder. "Not too bad, bounty man. You can ride the river with me anytime," she said, taking the tiller by herself.

"Thanks." Anthem grinned, wriggling life back into

his raw fingers and blistered palms. "I feel like I've been wrestling a buffalo."

"Beats swimming with them," Andy replied. She noticed McKane and Dollard and Wheatley returning from the bow. The men were drenched from riding the chute. Wheatley had lost a chunk of flesh where a splinter of wood had ripped his arm, but a hastily tied strip of cloth torn from his shirt had taken care of the wound.

"You boys make too much of a habit of going swimming in the winter, and you'll die of a cold instead of bullets," Cole told them.

"I reckon that snake venom DuToit calls whiskey'd go real good about now," McKane suggested and smacked his lips. "Looks like we made it, you old bag of leather and bones."

"Not by a long shot," Andy said, her eyes on the river. "The Rogue ain't done with us yet." Her gaze became distant, her speech measured, as if listening to the river. "The Rogue ain't done with us," she repeated. "And neither is Medicine Bear."

18

As before, the men drew straws for guard duty. Ben caught the last shift, the early hours before sunup. He was just as glad, that meant a good night of uninterrupted sleep, providing the Cheyenne cooperated. The ex-slave was snoring peacefully when Zack Hammond quickly descended the steps into the hold.

No one stirred. That gave Zack a feeling of power, to be the only one awake. He could do anything he wanted. His ruined nose began to throb, and he fixed his stare on Wheatley's sleeping form wrapped in a rough woolen blanket. He edged his way down the aisle, past Morgan, Dollard, the Irishman propped against a box of rifles, and DuToit, crumpled over his makeshift desk asleep and drooling on a hand-drawn map. He shifted his gaze to Anthem curled against the wall and then returned his attention to Wheatley.

Hammond's right hand opened and closed near his gun butt. He wanted to try his luck, shoot the black bastard and then ... what? Wind up in chains and brought to Fort Conrad for hanging? No. It had to look like redskin handiwork.

Zack nudged Wheatley with his boot. The black man rolled aside and aimed his Colt revolver at Hammond's belly. The gunrunner showed his hands were empty. Ben's gun had indeed caught him by surprise. His respect for Wheatley grew. He resolved to be more careful. The black man wasn't a tenderfoot anymore.

"There's a willow backrest and a couple of bearskin blankets up above," he curtly explained.

Ben nodded. He rubbed the sleep out of his eyes, yawned, and then using his Henry for a crutch, stood and headed for the stairs.

Outside, the night sky was ablaze with stars, its vastness bordered by the walls of the gorge rising a couple of hundred feet to either side. Bleak, soot-gray, rubble-strewn walls.

Ben glanced past the narrow railing on the larboard side of the boat, where a crude but serviceable raft rode alongside the keelboat, tightly secured to the larger boat by a length of rope. Cole Anthem had insisted they pull ashore after running the chute and build the raft. Ben couldn't see any reason for it. The worst of the journey was over; he couldn't see the keelboat sinking now. Andy herself had told them the big worry was the keelboat grounding herself on a sand bar where the Rogue ran shallow about an hour's journey ahead, where the Rogue cut a sharp dogleg southward.

Ben scrambled up to the roof. Standing, he studied

the pockmarked cliff rising into the darkness of early morning. Nothing seemed out of the ordinary. As for the river, the Rogue was an empty ribbon of reflected moonlight both upriver and down.

The keelboat rocked gently in the river's embrace. It was a pleasant sensation. And Ben decided, if the situation hadn't been so desperate the past few days, he could get to like river travel.

He heard his name whispered softly, Journey's voice. He turned to her as she joined him on the roof. She knelt on the buffalo robe and reached out her small slender hands to him. His trousers slid to his ankles with her help and he kicked free of them. He knelt beside her as she lay back and waited for him to undress.

He sat on his haunches to drink her in, the soft curves of her coffee-and-cream flesh, the small breasts and pointed nipples, the dark triangular shadow between her thighs. He kissed each breast. She tugged on his shoulders and pulled him to her hungry mouth, to the fire that burned within her. She consumed him, guiding him into the mystery of her passion, into the brokenness of her longing. She was a wave breaking on his shore, she was a wild animal he must tame, she was spirit and willful flesh, a teasing girl, a writhing wanton.

He thrust into her, pulled back, and almost lost the skin off his biceps as she clawed him and rose against him, desperate and demanding and then suddenly free, crying out and burying her face against his neck as the tremors, beginning deep within, coursed through every limb.

It was the same for him, and his dark hands entwined with her, and he wept for the beauty and the oneness they shared, at one wondrous moment that seemed like both dying and living.

She wanted to be open with him. She seldom allowed a man to know her in any more than the traditional pleasantries of a satisfied customer. But Ben Wheatley wasn't a customer. She had given herself freely, completely, and she wondered if she would ever again be able to pretend with another man. But who was she kidding? She would do what she had to in this world to survive.

She snuggled against him under the bearskin. He stirred and scratched her back. She all but purred in his ear.

"What happens after Fort Conrad," he asked, continuing to stoke her.

"I don't know," she said. "Maybe after the Cheyenne trouble's over with, I might try to get to San Francisco." She bit her lower lip. "Mmm . . . yes. I think I'd like Frisco." She traced a circle on his chest with her fingernail. His skin was smooth and warm. "What about you?"

"I'd like to see San Francisco," he replied. His hand squeezed her hip. "With you."

That was the right answer. She moved atop him, arousing him, sheathing his hardness and bringing the embers to flame once more.

* * *

"Are you asleep?" she asked, whispering.

"Yes."

"How can you answer if you're asleep, silly?"

"I'll think of an answer if you give me a moment."

"You are supposed to be guarding the boat."

"I am."

"With your eyes closed?"

"I listen better that way. Since it is too dark to see, I have to use my ears."

"Really?"

"Would I lie to you?"

"I've never known a man who didn't." She knew immediately that was the wrong thing to say. She wished she could take back the reference to her past . . . Too late. The words, once spoken, could never be recalled. Then again, why was she hiding, why? He knew what she was, what she had been, and might be again. And he accepted that.

Morning came early, with the gray of predawn. A shadow flitted soundlessly over the sleeping couple, followed by a coarse, ominous chuckle that woke them. The woman gasped, the man reached for his rifle.

"Hold it, boy," Zack sneered and cocked his revolver. "One wrong move and this'll be over a lot quicker than you'd like." He was standing on the roof, his back to the stern, legs splayed, an expression of triumph brightening his battered features. "Come out from them bear robes." He grinned and nudged the pelt with his boot. "Let's see what you got under there."

"Go to hell," Ben said.

"You first," Zack retorted.

Ben's eyes widened as the long, heavy barrel of a Henry rifle appeared past the edge of the roof and tapped Hammond on his inner thigh. Zack stiffened at the touch of the gun barrel and the smile slowly left his features.

"Drop it," Cole ordered, showing himself. He peered through Hammond's wide-legged stance at the couple wrapped in their bear robes. He shook his head in mock despair.

"It isn't what you think," Ben lamely said.

"Lord, but I hope it is," Cole replied. Sunlight was painting the river molten gold. He studied the cliffs and then tapped Hammond on the leg.

"Leave me be, you bastard. This is my business."

"Zack, you better put that gun away and get off the roof."

"Mind your own business. I've thought on it the whole night. Now I've made up my mind. A man has to see things through."

"Zack, I'd come down off the roof if I were you."

"You ain't me."

"Suit yourself."

Ben listened to the conversation, a bit incredulous at Cole's lack of concern for their safety.

"I'll wear your marks all the rest of my days," Zack said, staring at the helpless man and woman before him. "That ain't right. But I reckon I can balance the ledger right here and now."

A glint of sunlight reflected off metal, then a puff of smoke caught Zack's attention. His right leg jerked to the side, trailing blood and bits of bone. Hammond's roar of pain mingled with the distant bellow of a Sharps buffalo gun.

From his ledge overlooking the river, High-Backed Wolf knelt with his back to the granite outcropping he was using for cover. He crammed another shell into the breech and straightened, fired, dropped down, and reloaded.

Too ashamed for his earlier failures, he had sent another brave on to warn Medicine Bear that the keelboat contained the rifles and gunpowder the Red Shields so desperately sought. Now he loaded the buffalo gun and rose up to sight on the figures scurrying around the boat and fired again.

Wood splintered. A massive lead slug went whining off into the river. Ben and Journey rolled buck naked over the side of the roof and hastily pulled on their clothes, using the cabin for cover. Zack scrambled across the roof and dropped out of sight over the bow. Cole whirled and shot away the anchor rope, and the keelboat started moving sluggishly downstream.

Andy appeared in the doorway and made a lunge for the tiller. Cole ran along the runway and grabbed a pole. He was joined by Sergeant McKane and Sam Dollard, both with rifles in hand.

"We can't reach him with our guns," Cole shouted. "Let's get the hell out of here."

A head-sized chunk of the cabin wall exploded in a shower of splinters.

"Jesus Christ," McKane yelled, ducking in spite of himself.

Dollard turned and loosened a couple of shots from his Henry, wasting them as Cole had said. The range was too great even for the rifle. The sniper was at the crest of the cliff, poking over the rim to fire then disappearing.

Dollard cursed, grabbed a pole, and put his back into the effort. The keelboat increased its speed. Ben joined the effort and with four men working and Andy steering for the current, the keelboat soon left the gorge behind.

At the bow, Zack tightened a tourniquet around his right leg and stared with pain-glazed eyes at the ruptured flesh. That damn buffalo gun. It had killed Pa and Jay Lee and now it was after him.

From the cliff, High-Backed Wolf searched his buckskin pouch for more shells, but he had fired the last. The warrior stood and watched the keelboat pull away. He hung his head. He had done his best and he had failed. He had not stopped the escape of the *ve-ho-e*; he had not captured the repeating rifles and ammunition.

He turned and began walking from the cliff. High-Backed Wolf did not go to join the Red Shields. He would not share in their victory because he would not taint them with his bad medicine. He would return to the camp of his father and wait for Medicine Bear to return in triumph. And High-Backed Wolf would live in shame.

19

★

Medicine Bear waited in the cool shade of the pines. He waited apart from the sixty braves who had ridden their horses to exhaustion to reach this place. Here the shallow Rogue rounded a bend and then spread out. The water ran only as high as a horse's knee well out into the current. His braves would be able to ride up to the boat and swarm aboard. All he had to do now was wait.

He sat on a fallen tree and stared impassively at the surrounding forest, thinking of the victories he had already won. He had wiped out two detachments of soldiers and the camp of trappers. Many fresh scalps hung from his lance. Soon he would turn his warriors southward to the Yellowstone country. There he would ride at the head of his Red Shield warriors, fresh from his victories in the mountain country. The Cheyenne and Sioux villages would look on in envy and respect when he entered with the scalps of his enemies and bearing rifles and cartridges enough to arm many more than just his own warrior clan.

Medicine Bear could just imagine the many songs and stories his deeds would inspire. He smiled. He had a right to be proud. He had destroyed the *ve-ho-e*. Capturing the keelboat would make his triumph complete. And the cargo of repeating rifles would make the Red Shields invincible. Let his name then be written on the wind, for all time, Medicine Bear, war chief of all the Red Shields, a leader of his people, no slave to the white man's whiskey or the white man's ways. Soon, only the Cheyenne and their brothers, the Sioux, would walk the sacred hills.

Medicine Bear stood and strode from the forest and down the grassy bank that gave way to mud and gravel. There his warriors were gathered, all armed with breech loaders and some carrying revolvers. Though Medicine Bear decried the use of anything that came from the *ve-ho-e*, he made an exception when it came to the firepower of a Springfield breechloader or Colt revolver.

Nearly all the braves carried the rawhide shields, and a row of the twelve-foot lances had been thrust blade down in the mud, resembling a grove of limbless saplings.

Medicine Bear, his face crimson, his eyes wild and burning beneath the buffalo hat, continued out into the river.

"*O-he-estse!*" he shouted, raising his hand.

"River spirit.
Hear the cry of the
Morning Star people.

Bring our enemy to us.
Trick him, capture him
that we might take
many scalps. Though he begs us to spare him,
let the blood of the ve-ho-e
be carried downriver so
that all may know the
might of the Red Shields and
be afraid.
River spirit, daughter of the Above Ones. Hear me."

He turned around and found his men watching him.
Many of the young braves made no effort to hide the
fact they idolized him. But Sacred Horse and the older
warriors were more reserved in their appraisal. They
followed Medicine Bear because so far he had not
failed. He had shown good sense at times but even a
dog did that. Men like Sacred Horse had lived through
many battles and knew there was a difference between
being a skilled war chief and being a young wolf that
stumbles onto an injured buck and so makes a great
kill. The elders of the clan did not voice excitement
and fire their guns into the air or gather about Medicine Bear as he strode from the river.

Medicine Bear noticed the warriors who held back
but made no comment. He recognized his need for
them. Seasoned warriors were invaluable. But so were
enthusiastic ones. Wait until I have captured the river
boat, he told himself. Then they will know these
young braves have not misplaced their trust.

"Who is there to stand against us?" he shouted.

"None can stand against us," replied the braves around him, circling their war chief at the river's edge.

"My brothers, let us be quick in battle. We will fight with the courage of the wolf. Like the wolf, we will show no mercy."

"We will fight like the wolf," a chorus of young braves replied.

"Enough of talk" said Sacred Horse. He pointed upriver. "They have come."

Two hundred yards upriver, Andy Morgan's keelboat rounded a treacherous sandbar and cleared a line of spruce that grew close to the water's edge. The current was swift, the keelboat cut fast and steady through the water. From the boat sounded a mighty blast, a defiant trumpet call.

"Men will die today," said Sacred Horse as he walked into the woods to round up his horse.

"*Soa-voa-hey*! It is a good day to die," retorted Medicine Bear, marching past the weary veteran. The war chief of the Red Shields mounted and wheeled his horse in a gallop back toward the Rogue.

Sacred Horse caught the reins of his own half-wild stallion and swung up onto the animal's back. "It is never a good day to die," the warrior drily observed. And he rode to the river and the sound of battle.

20

"Sweet blessed Virgin!" Danny McKane said as the Red Shield warriors gathered downriver came into view. The trooper froze, his pole trailing in the river. The Cheyenne were massed on the shore. Their red-painted torsos were visible through a forest of twelve-foot spears. Lividly streaked war ponies danced as a chorus of terrifying whoops carried upriver and chilled McKane's blood.

"Steady on course," Andy said from the roof of the storage hold. Cole nodded and tried his best. Steering a keelboat was a lot like bulldogging a steer. You held on and prayed. Andy put the trumpet to her lips and once more sounded an earsplitting call that reverberated the length of the river.

"You crazy witch," Sam Dollard yelled, but Andy ignored his insult and climbed down to the tiller.

"Drop your poles and grab your guns," Andy shouted.

Cole didn't need to be told twice. He descended into the hold of the keelboat. Down below, Journey was using a barrel of black powder for a stool and busily loading a Henry rifle. She looked up at Cole, nodded, and resumed her efforts. Loading a Henry was a laborious process; the cartridges had to be fitted into a tube under the repeater's long barrel.

DuToit rose from his makeshift table. "Well then, monsieur, has the heathen arranged himself for the coming conflagration?"

"They're thick as ticks in the Ozarks, if that's what you mean," Cole replied.

"Well then," DuToit said and he slid the saber out of his sheath.

"That pig sticker isn't going to do you much good, Corporal. You better take a rifle."

"You may address me as captain," DuToit corrected in a tone ripe with long suffering. He held the curved blade up before him, slashed the air once, twice. "And may I suggest, since we shall all die today no matter how we struggle, that we fight as honor demands." He saluted and hurried up the stairs.

Cole shrugged. The man had a point. And if he wanted to fight and possibly die, why not as a captain?

"Is he right?" Journey asked, standing and buttoning the coat McKane had given her. "Are we all going to die?"

"We've survived everything else. Why not this?" Cole said.

"I used to not worry about it," she said. She brushed a long black strand of hair back away from her soft brown eyes and tilted her head up. "Living and dying were two sides of the same card. Toss it on the table, doesn't matter which side comes up. In my line of work you loose either way."

The trumpet blared again, startling her. Her hand tightened on the rifle and had it been cocked she would have blown a hole through the roof.

"Maybe neither of us will lose," Cole said. He stepped aside for the woman and allowed her to lead the way topside. "You go along, I've got to fix things here. It'll only take a minute." Journey didn't understand but she went on. She was anxious to meet whatever fate was in store for her with Ben Wheatley at her side.

Ben met her at the door and, putting his arm around her, lead her to the larboard side of the keelboat. The cabin wall would provide ample protection until the Indians swarmed over the boat. He told himself that wouldn't happen. And hoped he wasn't a liar.

A couple of minutes later, Cole emerged from the hold. He slung a bandolier of shotgun shells over Andy's shoulder.

"Much obliged," she said.

Cole looked downriver. The shallows were still a hundred and fifty yards off but the boat was picking up speed. He didn't like the way the sandbar intruded into the river. The boat would come to within fifteen feet of the mud. That's when the dance would really start. He tossed a box of cartridges to Ben and climbed up on the roof where McKane and Dollard were lying prone. DuToit was pacing the larboard side with Ben and Journey.

Cole passed extra cartridges to Dollard and the sergeant. "Where's Hammond?"

"Where he's been all morning. I tried to move him but he threatened to blow my fool head off so I let him be," said McKane.

"Sure is a waste of gold," Dollard interjected. He reached in his hip pocket for a faded yellow bandanna and blew his nose. His hand trembled, betraying his fear.

"I'd like to be rooting for potatoes in County Kerry now," McKane said with a sigh.

Cole patted him on the shoulder and slid down to the starboard runway and walked around to the bow. Zack was sitting with his back against the cabin, his gold pouch and a .45 in his lap. Though the tourniquet had stopped the flow of blood, his face was deathly pale. Cole had seen such leg wounds before, puckered flesh and jagged bone. They generally resulted in amputation.

"I'll carry you out of the way, Hammond," Cole said.

"Like hell you will." Zack cocked the Colt in his hand. "I'll do my fighting from right here." Zack coughed, groaned in agony and cursed. "Damn Sharps sure can make a mess. First Pa, then Jay Lee and now me. I shot Pa. He needed shootin' but that's not why I done it." Zack patted the parfleche of gold nuggets. "This is why I done it. But he needed killin'. Reckon I do, too. But I'll show you one thing. I'll show you a Hammond can die as much a man as any of you bastards. Now leave me be."

"Suit yourself, Zack." Cole saw nothing to be gained by arguing. "So long."

"Yeah. Be seeing ya!" Zack said.

Cole scrambled back up to the roof. He positioned himself near the stern, where he could protect Andy at the tiller. There was nothing to do now but wait, feel his gut tighten against his backbone and his mouth turn dry as sandpaper. He quit trying to count the Cheyenne braves. There were plenty, enough for each man to have his share. Her share, too, he corrected, thinking of Andrea Morgan and Journey.

His head began to throb. He reached up to massage his temple and touched the scar tissue from his self-inflicted wound, the ruse that had saved his life less than two weeks ago. The trick wouldn't work again. He had something else in store for Medicine Bear.

Cole peered out from the shading brim of his hat and thought he recognized Medicine Bear, the war chief himself, pacing his horse along the riverbank.

Be patient, Cole silently cautioned the warrior. The bounty hunter looked down at the Henry rifle. It wasn't the Yellowboy, but it would have to do. And suddenly the fear was gone, replaced by exhilaration. A cold smile spread across Cole's features. His big, rangy frame grew as taut as a spring; he exuded all the danger of a gun primed and ready to explode. It was only fifty yards to the Cheyenne now.

Ben noticed Anthem's expression, shuddered, and squeezed Journey's hand.

"You all right?" Journey asked in a worried tone.

Wheatley nodded. "I just wanted to reassure myself

there was still a little warmth in the world."

"If we get through this, I'll show you just how warm it can get," she said.

"We will," he tried to assure her.

The Red Shields charged out to intercept the keelboat. They opened fire from the bank and the sandbar. The Springfields were single-shot but had the greater range. Lead slugs began to pepper the boat.

"Ow!" Andy Morgan jerked to the side as a bullet shattered her right wrist while others spattered the wooden hull and beat a tattoo down the side of the hold.

"Fire!" Anthem shouted and he fired into the midst of the braves on the shore.

The rest of the men on the boat joined in on his signal. Each Henry carried a load of fifteen rounds. Wheatley, McKane, Dollard, and Cole fired as rapidly as they could work the lever-action repeaters.

The noise was deafening. Cheyenne warriors began to pitch from horseback. The water was churned to a muddy froth by riderless animals panicking before the constant fusillade.

Eager young braves charged the boat, firing as they desperately tried to end the murderous roar of the repeaters. The keelboat was drawing close to the sandbar; soon it would rush past on the crest of the rapid current. No brave seemed to be able to get any closer than ten feet from the keelboat before being picked off by the marksmen aboard.

While those around him emptied their Henrys as fast as they could, Cole chose his victims with methodical precision. He ignored what was happening all about him, immune to the confusion and the roar of the guns and the screams of the wounded and dying. He fired, shifted his aim, and fired again, concentrating on the next warrior in his sights and nothing else. For now that the killing had begun, nothing else mattered.

21

Smoke trailing from the barrel of his Henry, Cole drew a bead, exhaled, and squeezed the trigger, firing his last round. Sacred Horse groaned and clutched his side. Cole's bullet had ripped a hole through him just below the ribcage. He clung to his mount as the animal galloped out of the fray. Once on the riverbank, the warrior clumsily dismounted, dropped his rifle, and stumbled toward the forest. But he grew weaker with every step. His progress quickly grew more erratic. He fell to his knees and died.

The Red Shields streamed back from the river, nearly trampling Medicine Bear in their haste to escape such rapid-firing weapons. The war chief tried to shout above the din and rally his braves: But the noise and confusion was too great. No one could hear him. But his actions spoke volumes. He rode back and forth among his warriors, blocking the retreat, grabbing warriors and forcing them to turn and fight. Bullets cut the air all around him. Lead slugs clipped the rim of his war shield but miraculously missed him. His life was charmed.

Through sheer force of presence he stemmed the tide of his fleeing warriors. Even the braves who had reached the line of trees turned about, saw the valiant chieftain in the thick of battle, and, shamed by his example, loaded their Springfields and rode back to the river.

Medicine Bear took heart. He had turned his men into warriors again. But he watched in desperation as the keelboat, borne on a swift current, slid past the sandbar and irrevocably out of reach.

"*O-he-estse!* River spirit. Hear your child. Come to my aid," Medicine Bear shouted.

> "*We have offered you our blood.*
> *Do not allow these hated ones to escape!*
> O-he-estse. *I call upon you.*
> *Be with your people. Rise up!*"

Cole recognized Medicine Bear and sighted on him. Steadying the rifle, bracing himself against the storage hold, he adjusted for the swaying motion of the keelboat and slowly squeezed the trigger. Nothing.

"Damn," he muttered. He stepped back to reach for another rifle and noticed Andy Morgan for the first time since the melee had started. She was pale, her cheeks drawn and her eyes glazed with pain. She gripped the tiller between her left arm and her side.

Her right arm dangled uselessly at her side, her hand
covered in a glove of blood.

"I can't hold it!" Andy yelled. "We're too close. I
can't hold it!" She slumped to the left and swerved
the keelboat toward the Cheyenne-crowded riverbank.
Cole lunged toward the wounded woman and grabbed
the tiller.

He pushed with all his might and felt the keelboat
respond. Too late. The bow rose sharply, and the vessel shuddered as it pinned itself between two sub-
merged boulders hidden below the surface, Wood
groaned and splintered. Ben and Journey were
knocked sprawling on the runway. Ben pitched over
the side and landed square in the middle of the crudely
built raft tied to the boat. DuToit landed in the water
and emerged, sputtering and furious at the indignity.
He staggered onto a boulder.

Cole managed to hang onto the tiller, but the bolts
securing the keel broke loose and dumped him on top
of Andy Morgan, who was lying prone on the deck.

"Get off me, you lummox," she howled as her broken wrist was pinned by the bounty hunter's heavy
frame.

Cole rolled free and hurried to inspect the damage.
"Oh Goddamn!" he growled. The keel was indeed broken and could not function without being repaired.
The boat itself was securely imprisoned between two
smoothworn boulders like the jaws of a trap, only
forty yards downstream from the sandbar—and the
Cheyenne.

The Red Shields had momentarily ceased firing.

They stared at the boat in reverent silence, for many had heard the prayer of Medicine Bear. He had summoned the river spirit, and the spirit had obeyed his command, had captured the keelboat and the white men aboard. The horses would have to swim for the boat, but not far, and there were more than enough warriors gathered to provide cover for the first wave of attackers.

An eerie quiet descended on the river as Medicine Bear marshalled his forces. Fifteen braves quickly positioned themselves along the riverbank with others to keep those aboard the keelboat pinned down.

"Shit, we've bought it now," Danny McKane shouted. Medicine Bear walked his horse to the water's edge, where the bodies of the slain were being carried away by the current.

"Ve-ho-e," Medicine Bear shouted. "Hear my words." His voice echoed along the river and carried to the stranded keelboat.

Cole Anthem climbed atop the roof of the storage hold and, removing his hat, faced the war chief across the water and floating ice.

"What the hell are you doing, Cole?" Ben asked, climbing back onto the boat.

"Giving them something to think about," said Cole.

Medicine Bear recognized Anthem. The war chief felt an icy chill travel up his spine. This was powerful magic indeed. Many of the braves also remembered Cole from the battle, how they had circled him, how he had put the gun to his head and shot himself. Now he stood before them, back from the land of the dead to lead his white brothers to safety.

Who had the river trapped? they wondered. Were the *ve-ho-e* at the mercy of the Cheyenne? Or had the Red Shields been tricked by a prankster spirit into doing battle with dead men?

On the keelboat, Cole glanced aside and noticed the men were still reloading. He had to buy a little more time. He noticed Journey and called softly to her. She moved quickly to the stern.

"Bind Andy's arm. See if you can stop the bleeding and get her to the raft."

Morgan tried to protest, but her feeble entreaties were quickly overruled by Journey, who quite simply refused to listen to her. She helped the captain to stand and then led her to the raft. Andy managed to drag her sawed-off shotgun and the bandolier of shells. The raft bobbed beneath her weight, and she sank to the floor and lay prone.

DuToit pulled himself up from the rocks and onto the bow. Oozing red from a nasty cut above his eye, the Frenchman stared with a dazed expression at the bullet-riddled corpse of Zack Hammond. The gunman still held the gold he had murdered for and the Colt he had yet to fire. His head was tilted back and his jaw hung slack, his face frozen as in a silent scream.

DuToit wiped blood from his eyes. "You don't have anything to drink, do you?" he asked the corpse. "No. I thought not, monsieur." Philippe sat back against the wall of the cabin. And waited.

A shadow fell across him, then Sam Dollard

dropped down to the bow. He ignored DuToit and knelt by Hammond. He tugged on the pouch of gold, but the dead man clung to his treasure even in death. Dollard cracked the dead man's knuckles with the butt of his revolver and yanked the pouch free. He tucked the rawhide bag inside his shirt and hauled himself back up to the roof.

"What the hell would you be up to, Sam, my lad?" McKane asked.

"Mind your own damn business," Dollard growled.

McKane shrugged. Now was hardly the time to bicker. "What now, Cole?" he asked.

"I'm going below," said Cole. "Can you hold them off until I show up on deck again? Then we'll make our break."

"I'll hold 'em till Hell freezes over or you say different," said McKane. He spit in the palm of his hand, patted the Henry rifle, and winked.

"Where do you want me?" Ben asked.

"On the raft," Cole replied. "Grab a pole and be ready to shove us free."

"I can fight." Wheatley drew himself up in indignation.

"We aren't gonna stay alive by fighting," Cole bluntly retorted. "There comes a time to turn mother's picture to the wall and run. This is one of those times." He turned and studied the Cheyenne gathered around Medicine Bear. It was up to him to make the first move. He darted down to the hold.

On the sandbar, Medicine Bear looked at his men massed in the shallows. They awaited his command.

He studied the keelboat. The guns and ammunition it held were his for the taking. Such a prize was worth whatever the cost in life. How could he fail? The river spirit was with them.

And yet, dead men walked.

"I have come this far," he said beneath his breath. "I cannot go back. I will not go back and be called a frightened old woman who calls upon the gods yet fears when they answer."

He lifted his red shield and Springfield carbine high overhead. All eyes focused on him. "*Ne-ve-ohtsemestse*! [Come with me!]" His horse leaped into the current. A great war cry filled the air and the war party surged forward as one.

22

The war party plunged through the river in a shower of spray. Where it ran deep the horses were forced to swim, which slowed the onslaught and allowed the men on the boat to rip the ranks of mounted warriors with rifle fire. The Red Shields on horseback endured the fusillade and returned the gunfire. The braves lining the riverbank opened up and peppered the boat with round after round from their Army-issue Springfield carbines.

McKane cursed and ducked as a couple of slugs exploded against the hold inches away from the barrel of his Henry. The flattened bullets ricocheted harmlessly through the air. He glared at the men onshore, drew a bead, and fired. One of the Cheyenne on the riverbank howled and tumbled down a narrow incline into the water. He returned his attention to the three dozen warriors charging the boat. He sighted on Medicine Bear, fired just as a brave crossed in front of the war chief. The bullet slapped the unwitting brave from horseback.

"There's black luck for you," he muttered in exasperation. He sensed movement behind him, glanced over his shoulder in time to see Sam Dollard shimmy over the edge of the hold on the larboard runway. "Dollard!"

"Anthem can take care of himself," the scout yelled back as he headed for the raft.

"Stand with me, you bastard," McKane growled. He wormed around and crawled across the roof in an attempt to catch Dollard by the scruff of the neck and haul him back into line.

It happened fast. One moment McKane was grabbing for the treacherous scout, the next, a slug ripped through his left thigh. He groaned and whirled around. Two more bullets struck him in the shoulder and stomach and knocked him flat.

"Mother Mary," he muttered, disgusted with himself. "Danny McKane, you've gone and got yourself killed." He thought of Cole down in the hold. "Not yet, Danny boy-o, not yet."

He shoved himself upright, kneeling with the Henry rifle in his hand. He faced the braves as they swarmed toward the boat. He fired and fired again, turning in a slow arc. He blasted away at the Red Shields. One was as good as another, there was no point in aiming. The keelboat was an island in a sea of red-painted warriors with rifles and lances and rawhide shields and buffalo hats with blood-tipped horns.

The sergeant's wiry frame shuddered under the impact of bullet after bullet. He fired the last round from the Henry and tossed the rifle aside. He spat a mouthful of blood and reached for his holstered Colt. The movement threw him off balance and he fell forward on the roof, dying with his hand on his gun.

Sam Dollard leaped down onto the raft. Ben held the pole, ready to shove off as soon as the others were aboard. The scout brushed Journey aside and untied the line from the keelboat.

"Get us out of here," he ordered.

"Not without the others," Ben said.

"They're dead, you fool!"

"Cole isn't."

"Push off, you sonuvabitch," Dollard swung the rifle toward the mulatto. "Or I'll blow her pretty little head off." He cocked the rifle. "Now!"

"Don't do it," Journey said, squaring her shoulders. She didn't believe him. But Ben did. He braced the pole against the side of the keelboat and shoved the raft out into the current.

Sam snapped the Henry to his shoulder and shot a brave who appeared on the roof of the cargo hold and tried to bring his Springfield to bear on the raft. The Indian doubled over, clutched his belly, and fell back the way he had come.

The raft gradually slid away from the keelboat. The Red Shield braves lingering the shore noticed the craft as it left the cover of the keelboat and drifted into view. Bullets soon fanned the air around the raft and the human targets huddled low.

* * *

Cole tied three sticks of dynamite together with rawhide. He worked a blasting cap between the sticks and paused, listened to the roar of the Henry repeater rattle the roof overhead. He returned his attention to the task at hand. He took a chance and trimmed the fuse coiling from the makeshift bomb. Three sticks exploding simultaneously would set off the rest of the other crates of dynamite and the black powder, too. It ought to make a nice welcoming present for Medicine Bear.

He reached for the matches he had left on one of the crates and realized for the first time they were gone. The damn things must have been knocked from the crate when the keelboat grounded itself.

Cole straightened, not liking what he heard. The repeating rifles were no longer firing. And a red smear dripped, dripped, dripped from between the ceiling timbers.

Sweat beading his forehead, he crossed to the iron stove. He popped the trapdoor loose and, peering into the firebox, spied the fitful glow of a single piece of charcoal. He blew and got a faceful of ashes. He blew softly into the chamber, and watched the glow brighten.

He reached in with the dynamite and touched the fuse to the coal. The tip of the fuse began to sputter and trail smoke. Cole shoved the three sticks of dynamite down between two crates of explosives, covered the entire cache of weapons, powder, and shot with a tarpaulin, and ran back to the stairway at the stern of the keelboat. He bounded up the steps and leaped through the open doorway just as the Cheyenne began climbing aboard the boat.

A bloodcurdling screech sounded behind him. He spun and crouched low, brought his rifle to bear on a squat, muscular warrior on the roof. The Red Shield had waited, his spear poised, ready to skewer the white man when he appeared on deck. Now the brave desperately clawed a length of curved steel jutting from his chest.

The warrior slumped to the hold. Philippe DuToit dragged the saber free and saluted. Then he leaped down to the starboard runway to face the rest of the war party alone.

Cole spied the raft sliding away from the keelboat and Sam Dollard with his gun trained on Ben and Journey.

"The son of a bitch," he growled and ran toward the bow. He sensed danger behind him and flattened against the wall of the hold. A bullet fanned the back of his head, missing him by inches. He turned and fired. The Cheyenne was blown backward off the boat. Cole whirled to his right and fired again. The warrior rounding the bow dropped his breechloader and went sailing through the sunlight and splashed into the river.

Cole scrambled toward the bow, wincing as slugs struck the hold near his shoulder. He crouched by Zack Hammond's riddled corpse.

"DuToit! Come on!" Cole poked forward, rounded the bow, and fired into the warriors massed before the Frenchman. DuToit was slashing back and forth with his saber, the blade covered with blood and war paint. Wounded Cheyenne floundered in the icy current as they tried to reach the safety of the riverbank. Some were trampled beneath the horses and drowned.

Like wolves to the kill, the Cheyenne braves climbed over the stern. Some of them leaped to the roof. A brave knelt by Danny McKane and put a knife to the dead man's scalp line. Cole swung and shot the brave between the eyes.

A dozen Springfields at close range let loose a volley that slammed poor DuToit against the wall behind him. He pitched forward, landed on the back of a riderless horse, and flipped into the river.

Three braves scrambled to the roof and headed for Cole. Others dashed along the runway. The bounty hunter fired his last shot from his Henry, tossed the rifle aside, and dove through a hail of bullets into the river.

Sixty feet away, Sam Dollard watched in disgust as Cole surfaced and started swimming toward the raft.

Geysers of water spewed upward all around Anthem. He dove under the surface and swam for his life. Dollard cursed the poor marksmanship of the Cheyenne, and when Cole came up for air, he drew a bead on the bounty hunter. For one brief moment Journey was no longer under the gun. It was all the time Ben needed.

"No!" he shouted. He hoisted the pole from the river and, swinging it like a quarterstaff, brought one stout end down across the Henry. Dollard fired into the raft. Ben twisted and slapped the other end up alongside Dollard's skull. The scout flipped off the raft and fell headfirst into the cold gray-blue waters of the Rogue.

Ben wasted no time. He dug the end of the pole into the river, used it as a brake to slow the raft's progress, and angled the raft toward the opposite bank.

Cole continued to surface and dive until he neared the raft. But the gunfire had ceased. The Cheyenne had lost interest in him. They were too busy celebrating their victory. Andy Morgan's whiskey had been discovered and a jug was passed among Medicine Bear's men.

Cole kicked forward and swam for all he was worth. He had to gain the raft before the icy water numbed his muscles and he drowned. The raft rode the river, twenty feet away. Then fifteen. He continued to struggle. Within ten feet of the raft he began to lose his coordination and started to sink.

"Grab on," Ben shouted and stretched the pole out to him. Anthem reached out, caught hold of the wood, and held on for life as Ben dragged him to the raft and with Journey's help hauled him aboard.

"Thanks," Cole gasped and, trembling, managed to stand. He faced the riverboat and recognized Medicine Bear standing on the roof of the hold. The war chief of the Red Shields discarded his buffalo hat, picked up a Henry rifle, and held it aloft.

"Dead one. Do you run from me? Come back and I will kill you again!" he shouted across the water.

Cole walked to the edge of the raft and stretched

out his arms, offering himself as a target, more than
fifty yards from the keelboat.

"Are you mad?" Ben said and grabbed for Cole,
who pulled away. "We're in easy range of that
Henry."

Medicine Bear dug the rifle stock into his shoulder
and sighted along the barrel. He was oblivious to the
warriors climbing onto the boat and deaf to the noise
of their celebration. In his soul was stillness and calm.
Great was his victory today. He had accomplished all
he had set out to do. There was only one thing more.
The last act to make his victory complete. His finger
slowly tightened on the trigger.

The *Valhalla* exploded in a blinding flash and a
deafening roar that reverberated through the hills. A
gout of smoke pierced by a leaping flash of fire and
then an earsplitting blast and a shower of wood, water,
and grisly debris.

The braves along the bank were knocked off their
horses by the blast. The warriors lining the shore
stared dumbstruck at the carnage. Men screamed in
the river. The shrieks of the wounded and dying were
horrible. Those warriors not dead or wounded scattered into the forest.

On the raft, Cole turned to his companions. "If that
fuse had been an inch longer I'd feel pretty silly."

"You'd feel pretty dead," Ben corrected. Cole
couldn't argue with him.

At the opposite end of the raft, Morgan's eyes fluttered open. "I heard a noise," she moaned. She remembered being carried to the raft. "Where's my boat?"

"Oh, it's here and there," Cole replied.

23

★

Tomorrow they'd be at Fort Conrad. Cole intended to alert the troops stationed there and then buy himself the fastest horse he could find and enough provisions to last him to Denver. Glory ought to be healed enough for him to take her in his arms and carry her to bed. It was a pleasant reverie. A good one to hold on to.

"Don't seem right to blow up my boat and I don't even get to see it," Andy Morgan grumbled from the bedding of pine boughs Cole had fixed for her. She grimaced, turned on her side, and glared accusingly at the wounded arm that had failed her and caused her to run the keelboat up on the boulders. "If it hadn't been for this," she sighed, picking at the crude bandages securing her right hand, wrist, and forearm, "we'd be sleeping on feather beds and eating antelope steak at the Sutler House in Fort Conrad tonight." She grumbled something else but her voice died and she began to snore.

"Sounds like we'll make it for breakfast," Ben replied, feeding dry timber to the campfire. The blaze crackled merrily as it consumed the broken branches.

"I'll have a half dozen eggs," Journey added. "I know a lady who keeps chickens and supplies the officers. I'll have fried eggs and black coffee and maybe some biscuits." She sat upright, trying to appear feminine despite her ragged attire. "And I'll have a dress again and be rid of this ratty old coat." She tugged at the sleeve of the dark-blue woolen military coat that Danny McKane had given her. She brushed her hand across the sergeant's chevrons stitched to the sleeve. Her eyes grew moist. "No. I won't be rid of it. I'll keep it always."

The kind sergeant was dead. She missed him. Silas, too, with all his dreams. And poor DuToit, mad as a hatter from too much drink but valiant to the end. "So many dead . . ." She sniffed and wiped away the tears on her sleeve.

"Sometimes the way a man dies has to speak for his whole life," Cole said. DuToit had saved his life. McKane, too. Cole would remember. He hunkered down near the fire. The warmth of the blaze leached into his bones. It was a mild night, fragrant with the promise of spring.

Cole had chosen a campsite deep in the wooded grove, up from the river. The surrounding spruce and pine offered concealment. Even this close to Fort Conrad, he was taking no chances. A twig splintered in the darkness and he looked up sharply.

Ben hadn't heard the sound, but he noticed Cole become alert, like an animal poised to fight or flee.

"What is it?" Wheatley asked, keeping his voice low so as not to disturb the women.

Cole shook his head. He eased back on his haunches; his hand dropped to the Colt revolver riding on his hip. The black man across from him reached for his rifle and cradled it across his lap.

"It's probably just a squirrel or something," Wheatley said. "I mean, we're so close to Fort Conrad. And after the explosion, that war party didn't have any fight left. It's ended. Finished. Isn't it, Cole?"

The bounty hunter did not reply. Instead he stretched out on the boughs he had gathered for himself and covered himself with his buckskin coat. He turned his back to the fire, to allow his vision to adjust to the dark.

Ben muttered an expletive and gently bemoaned the fact that the world seemed full of uncommunicative bastards. He knelt where Journey had stretched out, covered her with his black frock coat, and snuggled against her for warmth. He kept his rifle close at hand.

Cole ignored him. His senses were alert now: sight, hearing, even smell searching the grove. It could have been anything, a squirrel, an owl, a white-tailed deer moving down to the river. Motionless, breathing easy and giving the impression of sleep, he waited, biding his time, giving the other three the chance to sink deeper into sleep.

It was ended? he wondered. There were a hundred innocent explanations for a broken twig. Unfortunately, it only took a single mistake to kill a man. Despite all the rational reasons, his instincts told him otherwise . . . the instincts of a hunter of men.

He stood, stretched, then looked at the huddled forms around him and walked from the campsite. He followed a winding path down through the woods, again plagued by the unmistakable sensation of being followed. He worked his way down a winding deer trail that lead to the Rogue River, its moon-dappled surface glimmering through the breaks in the forest. Thirty yards from camp the trail reached the riverbank and the raft they'd dragged ashore and covered with underbrush.

He continued on to the water's edge. He stared out across the river, listened, hearing the play of water on rocks, the rush of the river, of time itself speeding onward, each moment irretrievable whether lived for good or ill. Ben could probably come up with some fancy words to say about now, Cole figured. But no poet ever wrote more eloquently than the music of the river's flow; no artist ever dabbed with brush and oils a painting to compare with the shards of silver moonlight on the surface of the Rogue River.

Cole knelt by the water and leaned forward to cup a drink for himself. The water was cold and he splashed his face to wake himself up. He took his time, making himself a human decoy. He listened, and waited. Behind him, brush crackled, someone or something came running out of the thicket. He stood, drew his Colt, and thumbed the hammer back as he turned to face his assailant. A doe skidded in the soft earth as it leaped out of the woods and saw him for the first time. The animal tried to alter its course in

mid-leap and fell to its side. It jumped to its feet and
scampered down along the riverbank. He watched the
animal skirt the water. The startled animal bounded
over rocks and fallen trees as it made its escape.

"Well, I'll be damned," he chuckled and exhaled
slowly, the breath whistling between his teeth. He
turned to start back and came face-to-face with Sam
Dollard.

The scout knocked the gun from Cole's hand with
the broken shaft of a Cheyenne war lance. Dollard
reversed the spear and thrust the twelve-inch iron
blade at Anthem's midsection. Anthem only partly
blocked the thrust with his forearm. The blade left a
jagged wound in its wake. Cole stumbled backward,
lost his balance, and went down. The wild-eyed scout
leaped astride him and stabbed the spear at Anthem's
face. Cole caught the shaft just behind the blade and
held back the spear. Reflexes had saved his life. He
tried to catch his breath.

Sam Dollard brought his weight to bear. "Give it
up, Yellowboy. Give it up," he said through clenched
teeth. "You thought ol' Sam Dollard was a goner.
Look again. I rode me a piece of that keelboat right
on out of trouble. Followed the river till I seen the
campfire. Took a while for the feeling to come back
into my legs and arms. I knew my time would come."
The spear point dropped an inch closer to Anthem's
throat.

Cole brought every ounce of strength to bear and
twisted violently, unsettling the scout. Cole freed a leg
and kneed Dollard in the small of the back. The scout

fell forward as Cole twisted again and wrenched the spear free, knocking Dollard into the water.

Cole crawled into the shallows and caught Dollard as he tried to rise out of the water. He shoved the man's face back under the surface. His strong hands closed around the scout's neck.

"When you aren't running out on people, you're trying to murder them," Anthem gasped. He pulled Dollard up for air, then shoved him back again. The scout wasn't finished yet. His right hand broke the river's surface. Cole spied the rock too late.

Lightning exploded inside Cole's skull and he fell into the river. The cold water brought him back but he emerged with a goose egg-sized lump on the side of his head. For a few deadly seconds he was dazed, his movement slurred.

Dollard crawled on his hands and knees up from the riverbank. His progress was slowed as he spewed the river water from his lungs. He felt along the grassy bank, crawled another yard, and wiped the mud from his eyes. He spied Cole's revolver.

"Now, damn you," he gasped. He managed to stand, take a few steps, and fall forward over the revolver. When Dollard stood again, he held the Colt, spun, and cocked the .45. "Now!"

Cole rose on one knee, his right arm cocked and in his hand the broken spear. He threw it as hard as he could and fell forward, the roar of his own revolver ringing in his ears, the bullet ploughing harmlessly into the river.

Sam screamed. Like a wounded beast he screamed

and dropped the gun and clutched the shaft jutting
from his belly, the iron blade buried to the hilt in his
stomach. He screamed again and yanked the spear
free. He stared at the weapon, then dropped it. The
scout staggered past Cole, one shuffling step following
another down the riverbank, a dying man drawn to the
glimmering light.

He entered the water, clutching his belly as the surface rose to this knees, to mid-thigh. Sam Dollard settled facedown in the cold, glimmering rush of the
current that carried his lifeless body into the night.

"Now . . . it's ended," said Cole Anthem. Wearily
he stood, turned his back on the Rogue River. And
walked away.

HE LEFT HOME A BOY.
RETURNED A MAN.
AND RODE OUT AGAIN A RENEGADE . . .

TEXAS ANTHEM

KERRY NEWCOMB

AT THE BONNET RANCH, they thought Johnny Anthem had died on the Mexican border. But then Anthem came home, escaped from the living hell of a Mexican prison, and returned to find the woman he loved married to the man who betrayed him. For Johnny Anthem, the time had come to face his betrayer, to stand up to the powerful rancher who had raised him as his own son, and to fight for the only love of his life.

"Kerry Newcomb is one of those writers who lets you know from his very first lines that you're in for a ride. And he keeps his promise . . . Newcomb knows what he is doing, and does it enviably well."
—Cameron Judd, author of *Confederate Gold*

AVAILABLE WHEREVER BOOKS ARE SOLD FROM
ST. MARTIN'S PAPERBACKS

TA 12/00

SOME CALLED HIM THEIR CAPTAIN.

SOME CALLED HIM THEIR ENEMY.

SOME CALLED HIM THE DEVIL HIMSELF ...

MAD MORGAN

KERRY NEWCOMB

He came out of Cuba's bloody sugar cane fields, a young Welshman who had been kidnapped from his home and forced into barbaric slavery in the New World. Then on a black night, Henry Morgan made his escape, and soon was commanding a former prison bark manned by criminals, misfits and adventurers—men who owed Mad Morgan their freedom, their loyalty, and their lives.

"Awash with treachery and romance, this well-spun yarn fairly crackles with danger and suspense ... Colorful, old-fashioned adventure [and] vigorous historical fiction."
—*Booklist*

AVAILABLE WHEREVER BOOKS ARE SOLD FROM
ST. MARTIN'S PAPERBACKS